EAR TO THE
GROUND

EAR TO THE GROUND

PAUL KOLSBY AND DAVID L. ULIN
INTRODUCTION BY KAROLINA WACLAWIAK

un

The Unnamed Press
Los Angeles, CA

The Unnamed Press
P.O. Box 411272
Los Angeles, CA 90041

Published in North America by The Unnamed Press.

1 3 5 7 9 10 8 6 4 2

ISBN: 978-1-939419-73-6

Library of Congress Control Number: 2016933957

This book is distributed by Publishers Group West

Designed & typeset by Jaya Nicely
Cover illustration by Jaya Nicely

For Erik Himmelsbach, who believed.

INTRODUCTION

There is a certain comfort in knowing that although the Los Angeles landscape is always in flux—1920s art deco beauties morphing into 1960s atomic stucco apartments morphing into boxy glass condo monstrosities—the low-grade threat of an earthquake leveling all our architectural mistakes is ever present. In *Ear to the Ground*, which originally appeared as a serial in the *Los Angeles Reader* in the 1990s, David L. Ulin and Paul Kolsby put that threat and worry to good use. Capitalizing on potential catastrophe is a winning game in Hollywood, and in the hilarious *Ear to the Ground*, Ian, a struggling screenwriter who is reminiscent of many a struggling screenwriter in many a coffee shop in the Los Angeles Basin, wins the golden ticket of a million-dollar writing deal in the midst of The Big One's imminent arrival. The novel is a commiseration on the excess of the 1990s, when screenwriters like Joe Eszterhaus were scoring multi-million dollar deals and directors like Michael Bay and Roland Emmerich were making their stamp on Hollywood with bombastic disaster films like *Armageddon* and *Independence Day*.

The 1990s also offers some of our most enduring cinematic visions of Los Angeles and Hollywood. The Coen Brothers' masterpiece of a screenwriter's Hollywood hell, *Barton Fink*, carried on a long tradition of Hollywood send-up novels like Budd Schulberg's *What Makes Sammy Run?* and Nathanael West's *The Day of the Locust*. These tales of terror are still handed out to eager film school students on their first day and provide more of an education about the wherewithal necessary for a spot on the lot. Necessary too, upon arrival to a Paramount-adjacent studio apartment, is a viewing of the quintessential Hollywood send-up, *Swimming with Sharks*. Working an agency desk for a week could surely get the first glimmers of anyone's vengeful reverie going, even now. But the believers still keep coming, enduring humiliation and despair for a chance to grab the brass ring of fame. *Ear to the Ground* carries on the tradition of these acerbic Hollywood satires as starry-eyed earthquake specialists are caught in the web of disaster movie-making with excitable D-girls, alongside cameos from bad boy European super directors.

Like William Faulkner, Joan Didion and Bruce Wagner before them, writers have long been wading into Los Angeles's literary waters, myself included. One has to deeply love the strange, lonely pulse of the hidden neighborhoods and haunted canyons and be on the right vibration to "get" Los Angeles and write about it with credibility. It's a vibration I struggled to tap into over my years in Los Angeles, but I feel lucky to have found it—in all its peculiarity and sunny doom. There's a reason writers flock here and a reason I couldn't stay away (five years in New York was all I could muster): Los Angeles is a city of perpetual hope and chance, a 24/7 Vegas casino with a bright sun and glittering blue sky, and a place where reinvention is still an ever-present dream.

There's an exciting nostalgia that wafts through *Ear to the Ground*—nestled between the moment Jerry Garcia died and O.J. Simpson's trial for murder began—and though Ed Debevic's and Damiano's are gone from our grid, it's nice to revisit a time when million dollar movie ideas were still being written down on bar napkins.

— Karolina Waclawiak

A NOTE ON THE TEXT

Ear to the Ground was originally published as a weekly serial novel in the *Los Angeles Reader*, beginning with Volume 17, Number 30, May 5, 1995 and ending with Volume 18, Number 17, February 2, 1996. An additional chapter not published in the *Los Angeles Reader*, "Charlie in Kobe," appears here for the first time as an appendix. Minor inconsistencies in the narrative that occurred during the process of serialization have been left intact.

EAR TO THE GROUND

LOS ANGELES IS THE ONLY MAJOR CITY IN THE WORLD, thought Charlie Richter, heading east on Sunset in his red Rent-a-Corsica, where everybody has to drive. The May morning sun was a laser, confounding even the most creative extensions of his car's visor, so he looked over at the bus to his right, moving along with him at eleven feet per minute. Its passengers seemed uniformly unhappy, and it occurred to him that Detroit had planned its L.A. marketing campaign carefully. *Drive* and you'll be happier.

When traffic began moving freely, Charlie spilled his coffee to the tune of a drop at La Cienega, a splish at Fairfax, and a thwap at La Brea. He took a right—going south—determined to avoid left-hand turns of any kind. La Brea was straight and simple and easy to maneuver one-handed. The red light at Melrose introduced him to a pretty blonde, around thirty, alone in a spanking white Honda Accord, howling with laughter. She caught him noticing and lowered her passenger window. "Howard Stern," she giggled.

"What?"

"On the radio. Howard Stern."

The light turned green and he saw no more of her. Turning again, he made his way along Oakwood, past its stucco apartment buildings that appeared to have been shaped from a single mold. He noticed the cracks in their exteriors—at the corners usually, and extending diagonally and horizontally from the windows. Apparent also were the patch-jobs, where wet concrete had been slung as caulk and had discolored quickly.

Charlie pulled into a permit-only zone in front of 418 North Spaulding where, twelve minutes later, he received a thirty-five-dollar ticket. He was, meanwhile, scratching plaster from the house's front wall with a Swiss Army knife and mixing it on the palm of his hand with a bluish liquid he squeezed from an eyedropper. Satisfied with his findings, he walked around to the north side of the building, looking for a way into the basement. He discovered a crawl space, which, with a shove of the grate, he easily entered.

Louis Navaro intended to rise early and wash his car in front of the building he owned. He had given the Santa Ana winds nearly two days to swirl their desert dust around his quarter-panels and work their insidiousness into his MacPherson struts. A bucket of hot water and a serious gob of Latho-Glaze would stun the demons, and force their retreat. It was his building; it was his car. The woman who'd left him seven years earlier had taken everything else—except for a duplex he'd converted from two vertically stacked apartments, blasting through the ceiling of the lower in a surge so libidinous he was convinced it was the sort of gesture to make her stay a lifetime.

He was wrong, of course, and after two years he moved into a smaller unit on the other side of the building, hoping the duplex would be easy to rent, in spite of its price: twenty-four hundred dollars, *firm*.

Currently, he lay in bed, staring at a tiny crack in the ceiling that resembled the depiction of a river on a map. He'd had a dream about a cruise boat that sailed, curiously, from Los Angeles to Chicago. The rest was pretty hazy, and no amount of recollection served him. So when at first there was a scraping sound beneath him, he didn't notice. It persisted, however, and became a *pop-pop*, then a *cack-cack*, so Navaro got up. He jumped into some khakis and, zipping up his fly, went out the front door, and around to the side of the building.

Only Charlie's feet and ankles were visible. Navaro, barefoot and barechested, took note of the exposed black leather uppers and the conservative-looking trouser cuffs. He paused for a moment before he heard from within the rap of metal on metal.

"What're you doin' there? Hey!" The rapping stopped.

"Hello? Mr. Navaro?" The voice was muffled.

"Who's that?"

"It's Charlie Richter." It sounded like "Cawa Rawa." Gradually, the ankles led to shins, and thighs. Charlie's white button-down emerged, smudged. The expression on his face resembled that of an auto mechanic with bad news. "I was checking the foundation."

"The *foundation*?"

"I was wondering why there's no X-brace along the front."

"What?"

"Front to back, the expanse is X-enforced, but along the front it's only an H, and then kind of a …"

"Hey, I'm tri'na find a tenant, not a building inspector."

"No, I mean …"

"Whaddya afraid of? The Big Bad *Wolf*?"

Charlie smiled and stood up.

"This building got through Northridge, nothin' happened."

"Uh-huh." Charlie brushed some pebbles from his trousers and looked over at the lawn. "What was your price again?"

"Twenty-four hundred, *firm*."

"Two thousand."

"No way."

"Tell me," Charlie hesitated, "how long's it been vacant?"

Navaro lit a Pall Mall, and spat out a fleck of tobacco. He took a couple of drags and looked his prospective tenant in the face. "This is the only duplex in the neighborhood."

"Precisely." This somehow put the landlord at a disadvantage. "Nobody wants to pay that much rent around here."

"It's a damn good neighborhood. And a damn good apartment."

"At twenty-four hundred, people want to live in Beverly Hills."

"Whaddya need so much space for?"

"My equipment."

There came the pause that accompanies any derailed negotiation, until one side or the other realigns it. In this case, it was Charlie.

"Here's what I'm saying. I'd like you to think for a minute about my next offer, and if you can't abide by it, just say no, and I'll wish you the best."

Navaro dropped his cigarette. Charlie, seeing the landlord's bare feet, squashed it cold, and continued: "But if you say yes, we'll be in agreement, which makes sense, since we'll be living under the same roof. So, if it's all right with you, I'd like you to think carefully before answering."

"All right."

"You'll think about the figure I'm about to give you?"

"Yeah, yeah," Navaro answered impatiently.

"Two thousand."

Grace Gonglewski swallowed the last sip of her coffee and put the cup on the kitchen table, in the center of the patch of sunlight that drifted in through the triple row of windows over the sink. She glanced at the script tented beside her, then looked at her watch. Eight fifty-four. I'll finish this tonight, she thought, and then she let the pages fan themselves shut with a breeze that ruffled the tiny hairs on her forearm. Ruefully, she glanced toward the high-ceilinged expanse of the living room, where two waist-high stacks of screenplays sat next to a white Ikea couch.

Each day at Tailspin Pictures seemed like a lifetime to Grace. She felt, every morning—usually at the intersection of La Brea and Hollywood, where that chrome sculpture reminded her of New York—that she would die in Los Angeles, probably at Warners, reading at her desk.

They wanted her to plow through three thousand pages of screenplay format every week, identifying gems. But God help her (He didn't) if what she thought was a gem turned out to be coal, or—according to Ethan, two years her junior—shit. She had not the power to say yes at Tailspin Pictures; neither actually did her boss. Grace lived and marched in the ranks of Development, and it was her job to say no.

If all that was something of a crapshoot, however, Grace's apartment, at least, was hers alone, created in her own image, where she answered to no one but herself. Looking at the pattern of sun and shadows coming through the curtains, she felt, not for the first time, as if she couldn't bear to leave. Then she went to get her sunglasses and keys.

The bedroom was mossy, dark, a tangle of sleep smells, crumpled bedclothes and curtains drawn against the light. As Grace's eyes adjusted, she grimaced at the mess. Sprawled across the width of the queen-size mattress lay Ian, hand raised, as if in protest, against the headboard's knotty pine. God, *Ian*—she'd forgotten all about him, although it should hardly have come as a surprise. In three months, they had never once had breakfast together, and lately, she'd even given up kissing him good-bye. Looking at one skinny, dark-haired leg protruding from the sheets, she felt a small finger of revulsion tickle the back of her throat, and she had to fight off the urge to kick him, to tell him to go on home where he belonged. Then she noticed the delicate architecture of his back and, as his breathing rose and fell in small crescendos, her revulsion faded into a shimmering aura of desire.

Outside, the sun was bright but not hot, and morning mist hung like vapor in the air. As usual, Navaro was sitting at the bottom of the front steps, staring at his 1979 Le Sabre as if it were a limousine. When Grace passed, he raised his head and leered at her, sunlight reflecting like lightning off his oiled black hair.

"Guess what?" he said, eyes on her breasts. "I rented the place."

It took a moment, but then Grace saw the open doorway behind him, and understood.

"Really?" she said. "To who?"

"Some guy," Navaro explained. He took a quick look over his shoulder before cocking his finger to his ear and moving it around. "He's a little strange, you know? Asking me about the foundations, shit like that. But hey"—he raised his palms to the sky in an exaggerated shrug—"he paid me three months' rent, up-front."

"I'm sure he'll be fine," Grace said, not really caring but wanting to be polite. Still, she lingered, the glimmer of a question flickering at the edges of her mind. "He's not in the entertainment business, is he?"

"Depends on how you define entertainment. He says he's a scientist, whatever that means."

The first thing Charlie did inside his new apartment was to hang his suit and dress shirt in the upstairs hall closet. Then he walked off the dimensions of the place, jotting his findings in a blue pocket notebook, and trying to picture how it would look after his machines had been installed.

In the master bedroom, Charlie looked out the windows at the overgrown backyard. Beyond it lay a high chicken wire fence and the back of another house. He didn't know much about the neighborhood but, Charlie thought, it didn't matter; the only important thing was that he was here. He could taste the excitement, a flavor in his mouth. He took a deep breath, and another. Then he went into the bathroom and let the old stall shower run.

For as long as Charlie could remember, the feeling of running water on his body had calmed him, had helped him sort out his thoughts and clear his emotions. Today was no different—until he stepped out of the shower only to realize, too late, that he did not have a towel. For a moment, he stood there, helpless, but then he shrugged, and shook himself off like a dog. Water splattered everywhere, fanning out like the cracks left behind by an earthquake … and suddenly, Charlie was seeing the connectedness of the pattern, each drop linked to the ones around it. He closed his eyes and tried to imprint the vision but, like some abstract notion, the floating image would not coalesce.

So Charlie walked naked through the apartment. Briefly, he considered getting dressed, but it was still too early, so instead, he carefully laid out his clothes on the hardwood floor and sat down to meditate. Slowly, painfully, he folded his legs into a lotus position and let his eyes unfocus on a spot across the room. He drifted, but only until a driving bass line began to rumble through the wall from the apartment next door, followed by a fuzzed-out electric guitar, and the steady snap of a bass drum and snare. Although Charlie tried to ignore it, within seconds, there was nothing in his head but noise. Christ, he sighed. Then, refocusing his eyes, he extricated himself from the lotus and went for his clothes.

In the middle of the spare white expanse of Grace's living room, Ian was in his boxer shorts, rocking back and forth to Courtney Love. He had only been out of bed for five minutes or so, but already the day was beginning to unveil its charms. The bag he'd stashed in the battery compartment of his laptop had yielded exactly one joint, and now he stood smoking and swaying, the sun glancing off his back and legs like a lover's caress, muscles melting into languid liquid, and the edges of the world going all woolly, as if a layer of green gauze had been laid across his eyes.

Ian noticed the stacks of scripts next to the couch, and he felt himself drawn. A month before, he'd given Grace an old screenplay of his and asked about rewrite work, but although she had smiled and said she'd see what she could do, he'd had the feeling that his request had made her uncomfortable, and he was wary of bringing it up again. He did, however, wonder about the competition, and staring at the piles, he felt his bowels tighten with the incipient thrill of illicit snooping. Grabbing a script, Ian flipped past the title page—*Web of Sin*—and turned quickly to page one:

EXT. DARK NEW YORK STREET — NIGHT

Let me guess, he thought, I'll bet there's a gunshot somewhere in here. He scanned down the page until he found one. Then, nodding to himself in satisfaction, he put the screenplay back, not noticing that the head had fallen off the joint and burned its way through the first few pages, leaving a small, but noticeable, scar.

Ian booted up his computer at the kitchen table and ground some beans for coffee, leaving a residue on the counter near where the filters were stored. He took a final hit off the joint and squeezed the roach into the watch pocket of his jeans, then popped two slices of bread into the toaster. Once the toast was singed brown as a Malibu hillside, he slathered on some peanut butter and began to eat, standing there without a plate, crumbs falling to the floor like flakes of ash.

After the coffee was ready, Ian sat down and adjusted the contrast on his laptop. He was working on a new screenplay, and now he opened up the file, enthralled as the words emerged like magic on the screen. He scrolled back five or six pages, watching the sentences appear and disappear as he retreated to the middle of Act Two. The script was at a critical juncture, he realized, and he'd been working around the issue for days, spinning scenes that didn't go anywhere, that took up pages and pages without moving the story along. He had his characters together, but somehow they kept walking off in their own directions, and when it came to the earthquake with which he wanted to end, everything he'd written seemed like a cliché.

Man, Ian thought, this is too much. Maybe I should do something else, and start to write when my buzz wears off. For a moment, he just sat there, his mind as blank as the morning light. Then he unhooked the phone and plugged the cord into the back of his computer, making sure to deactivate Grace's call-waiting before dialing America Online.

At eleven fifty, Charlie entered the ballroom at the Four Seasons Hotel and searched out Sterling Caruthers, who promptly fixed his colleague's tie by tightening its knot. Already, journalists were scurrying around like noxious bugs, bearing press credentials from newspapers, magazines, radio, and TV.

"Nice of you to join us, Mr. Richter," Caruthers said, his voice dripping blood. The press conference would begin in ten minutes.

"I'm sorry. I ..."

"Never mind." Caruthers dismissed him with the wave of a hand. Charlie would be seated, he was told, at the far end of the dais, where it was unlikely he'd be called upon to speak. Once there, he began an entanglement with a heavy velvet curtain, which not only obstructed part of his chair but obscured his microphone, as well. He tried pushing the curtain backwards, and then forwards; finally, having no other choice, he slung the thing around his neck and wore it like a shawl.

Charlie's new employer, the Center for Earthquake Studies, or CES, was endowed with a multimillion-dollar budget rumored to have come about, in part, through a hushed yet symbiotic relationship with the entertainment industry, whose interest lay in the Earthquake Channel, as well as an interactive TV series called *Rumble*. "If the Big One hits L.A.," mused an inside source, "the studios will be in on the ground floor."

There was dissent; the Caltech people were up in arms. The mixing of science with commerce, they claimed, would make it impossible for pure research to take place. Caruthers begged to differ. As CES's nonscientific figurehead, he'd engaged the services of Gold & Black, a pair of entertainment publicists who had called this press conference and guaranteed a respectable turnout from journalists and other notables—in return for ten thousand dollars.

The first difficult question came from Maggie Murphy of the *Los Angeles Reader*, who asked Caruthers whether CES had enough scientific vision to warrant spending so much money. Caruthers answered feebly. When pressed with a follow-up, he shot back a question of his own: "How much money is too much?"

"It all depends on what you intend to do with it," Murphy said. "Do you know that the Caltechies are calling you guys CESSPOOL?"

"That's their business," Caruthers announced. "Ours is to develop techniques that will enable us to predict earthquakes with enough time and accuracy to save the city of Los Angeles and other municipalities considerable expense and loss of human life." He fixed Murphy with a take-that glare.

But Murphy had done her homework. She was Lois Lane with a metallic toughness. "I assume Dr. Richter will be involved in this prediction effort?" Caruthers nodded. "Then why," she went on, "do you have him over there behind a curtain?"

Embarrassed, Charlie unraveled himself, while a hotel employee held the curtain aside.

"You're Charles Richter, right?" Murphy asked in a staccato voice. "Grandson of the Richter scale Richter?"

"Yes," Charlie mumbled.

"And you predicted the quake in Kobe, Japan?"

Camera crews adjusted their positions, and lights were aimed at Charlie's eyes. He stared into them, looking for a face, but all that came back at him was an aurora of white.

It was true, if not very well known, that Charlie, who'd been traveling for research and for escape, had been in Kobe at the time of the earthquake, giving a paper called "Fault Lines: The Mystery of Plate Tectonics" at a seismographic conference in nearby Osaka. Strolling along the banks of Osaka Bay, shoes in hand and trousers rolled to the knee, he'd noticed something irregular about the tide-flow. After testing water samples, Charlie studied the data—blocks of numbers—and felt a sudden nausea. He took a taxi to a grassy hillock and noticed birds flying overhead in strange configurations. Then he removed a stethoscope from his knapsack and, for more than an hour, kept his ear to the ground. At dinner, he mentioned to a colleague in passing that metropolitan Kobe sat on a tectonic boundary in the process of shifting. Later, drinking Burmese whiskey in his room, he noticed an undeniable correlation between two disparate columns of numbers. He dialed his colleague's extension and arranged to meet him in the hotel bar, where he explained that Kobe could go at any moment. The man laughed in Charlie's face and spread the word to some other seismologists, who reacted similarly, behind his back. Twenty-four hours later, no one was laughing.

Maggie Murphy stood now, as did the *Times* reporter and the guy from ABC. Sterling Caruthers hadn't opened his mouth in half an hour, as Charlie, blithely sipping from a glass of water, more or less became the subject of these proceedings, deflecting and focusing the debate, explaining technical principles in layman's terms. Finally, he and Caruthers exchanged a meaningful but complicated glance. Things were winding down.

"What are your present plans, Mr. Richter?" asked Murphy with a smile.

"I go where the promise of seismic activity exists."

"Yes?"

"And I've just taken an apartment in Los Angeles."

THURSDAY NIGHT

YOU CAN FIND THEM BY THE BAR, OR IN THE BACK booths of the last room at the Formosa on Thursday nights, where there's no smoking until ten-thirty, after which the waitresses couldn't care less. Just half a year ago, they went to Dominick's off San Vicente—slews of them from Fox and Paramount, and from Sony—but when Dominick's faded out, and the Olive dissolved into Jones, everyone cut to the Formosa. Among studio youngsters, Friday has always been Hangover Day.

Grace watched Ian peeling off his Budweiser label at a table across the room, while two girls sitting next to her— an agent's assistant and a VP (in title only)—admitted freely that they'd fuck him at the drop of a hat. Women liked Ian, which exhilarated Grace because it made her nervous, but it disappointed her that, as a result, she felt more attracted to him. Was he better on paper, she thought, or in bed?

Ian was in good form just then. "Imagine," he said, "if we had interactive cameras in our living rooms, right?" His whole table listened. "And there was an earthquake, and some computer geek, in *Iraq* for chrissake, could watch our TVs smashing and our books falling out of the shelves, and paintings coming off hooks; and us walking in, rubbing our eyes, checking our limbs, freaked out but alive, as the car alarms are going off and the dogs are howling and soon everyone around you is awake ..."

"Nobody's putting a camera in my living room," announced a former writing partner.

"Why not? Everybody'll do it. Or mostly everybody."

The others seemed unsure.

"Look at it this way," Ian continued, "a hundred years ago, Bell was shouting into this archaic telephone: 'Watson, can you *hear* me?' Now we have voice-mail, and car phones; we hang up on each other, and Star-69. *Two* hundred years ago"— he was on a roll now —"if you wanted to listen to music you either played it yourself, or you heard someone else playing it. I mean ..."

"That's true," said a guy from Fox.

Ian leaned back, satisfied with himself. Fox thinks I'm smart, he thought. He thinks I'm smart, and he'll probably hire me—not right now, but down the line. In for a penny, in for a pound. Life is *long*. Grace came over then and scooted next to him, put her arm around him, and smiled to the others. He liked the way she smelled. She crossed her legs, making sure to pull down her skirt. She was pretty. That wouldn't hurt him at Fox, either.

Ian's father still sent him two thousand a month, so he ordered another beer and one for Grace. A guy named Marcus began to talk about his new script—the dreadful tale of an airplane, a bomb, several black nuns from Detroit, and an ex-New York City cop. Meanwhile, under the table, Ian ran his hand lightly up Grace's thigh. She tried to take it seriously—the story— because this twenty-three-year-old schmuck, Marcus, sold a spec last month to Joel Gold and was at the top of the B-list.

However, by the time the SECOND NUN pulled an assault rifle on the hijackers, Grace was turned on. Ian had worked his way to her hip, fiddling with the elastic at the edge of her panties and watching her smile. Then he excused himself, went to the bathroom, and rolled a joint, which they smoked alone together in the parking lot, stealing kisses between hits, leaning against the rear quarter-panel of an old Ford Bronco parked in a space marked Ethel Waters. Across the street, a dark figure hustled toward Jones, a valet. He would make a fine character, Ian thought, and he and Grace kissed deeply for a moment, probing like scientists with their tongues.

Charlie heard them come up the stairs, laughing and drunk; he heard their voices soften as they got inside her apartment, and when they came into the bedroom he heard them rise again as sighs and moans, a steamy call-and-response through the hollow wall. On the floor in front of him, two laptop computers exchanged data; their screens cast an eerie, underwater light. They're screwing next door, Charlie thought, as he picked up the dog-eared address book by his side and reached for the phone. Flipping through the pages, he wondered who'd mind least if he woke them up.

THE GIRL NEXT DOOR

CHARLIE KEPT THINKING ABOUT THE GIRL NEXT DOOR. Ever since the night he'd heard her, like a Santa Ana wind through the bedroom wall, he had found her entering his mind at odd moments: in the supermarket, for instance, or while staring at a computer screen. He wasn't obsessed—he had never even *seen* her, for Christ's sake—just a little, well, curious, if that was still something people felt in this day and age, where everything was up for grabs and yours for the taking, if only you knew better than to ask.

This morning, as he left his apartment, checking to make sure he had turned both locks, Charlie glanced across the landing at her door. The day was silent, the sun as white as movie light.

On the sidewalk, Navaro dragged a dirty rag soaked in sudsy water across the hood of his Le Sabre.

"So tell me," he asked Charlie. "You renting that thing by the week?"

"Pardon?"

"The car." Navaro nodded at the red Corsica parked across the street. When Charlie didn't answer, the landlord straightened up and wrung his rag out on the ground. "Never mind. You meet Grace yet?"

"Pardon?" Charlie felt like he was missing something, like he didn't understood the words.

"Grace." Navaro looked at him though hooded eyes. "She lives next door to you."

"Grace?"

Navaro laughed and kicked his right front tire.

The Center for Earthquake Studies occupied a former sound stage on Culver Boulevard just west of Overland, catty-corner to the Sony Pictures Studios. Big and boxy and windowless, the building was painted a stucco shade of tan.

Inside, an arched ceiling hung above the space like a dome of sky, reminding Charlie of a beehive. He nodded hello to a couple of faces he thought he recognized, and moved quickly across the room to a locked, unmarked door.

It was always the same in the Prediction Laboratory, a subtle shade of twilight, quiet beneath the ever-present electrical hum. With its computer models and maps marked with pushpins tracing earthquake activity, the lab reminded Charlie of a command center, more military than scientific. Kenwood was already at his desk, staring at the wall above it as if deep in thought. Charlie didn't want to disturb him, but then he realized Kenwood wasn't working, just looking at a picture of a dark-haired woman. "You should really take it down," Charlie said, his voice as even as the wind.

Kenwood didn't move. His face looked normal, except for the mouth, cut into an exaggerated mask. "You know what the thing of it is?" he whispered. "I keep thinking that in twenty years, she'll just be someone I loved when I was young. I won't even remember her. She'll be obsolete."

"People die," Charlie said.

"We were married one year."

"It's not your fault."

"What's not his fault?" Charlie turned to see Sterling Caruthers standing in the door. Caruthers was the only other person with a key to the lab, and he made it a habit to show up unannounced, peering through microscopes and at computer screens as if he knew what he was looking for.

"Nothing," Charlie said.

"What did he do?"

"It's personal, OK?"

"What did you do?" Caruthers folded his arms across his chest and glared at Kenwood.

"We were just talking," Charlie told him.

"You should be working. What about Indio?"

"Indio was nothing."

"There were two temblors less than a mile apart."

"Tremors like that happen all the time out there."

"Listen," Caruthers said, "if you don't think Caltech's getting ready to make a prediction of its own … "

"Sterling," Charlie said again, "those quakes don't add up to a thing."

"Then it's your job to *make* them add up. We are here to predict an earthquake, gentlemen. Now, if we mark a course from Indio up to L.A. … "

Caruthers sat down at Kenwood's work station and began to tap at the keyboard. On the screen, a map of Southern California took shape, a latticework of fine green lines. Charlie stared at it for a moment, thinking there was something delicate in its construction, a fragile balance similar to that of the earth itself. Certainly, he thought, there had to be a way to read that balance consistently. But it would take time to find.

Caruthers's voice droned on and on as he plotted points on the computer, and Charlie stopped listening, hearing it as if through a wall. It was like a sound that came at him from the other apartment. In the last week, there had been lots of noises, and once he thought he'd heard someone in the hall, but it was only a cat scratching at his doormat, looking for a place to get warm. Charlie tried to concentrate on what Caruthers was saying, but he couldn't stop thinking of the girl next door.

MEETING OF THE MINDS

IAN WAS ALONE IN GRACE'S BEDROOM WHEN THINGS started to get weird. First the lights went out, then the darkness seemed to harden into solid particles. There was a moment of utter stillness, the most vivid stillness Ian had ever known, before a rumbling erupted all around him, the floor and walls and ceiling began to shake, and he felt himself going down.

Ian sat bolt upright, eyes blurred and rheumy, his face a greasy mask of sleep. Slowly, he took in the familiar surroundings: the wicker chair in the corner, the comfortable clutter of his clothing on the floor, and a pile of scripts— Grace's weekend reading—by the bed. He put his hands out beside him, patting down the mattress as his breathing calmed. Solid, he thought. It was just a dream.

Suddenly the ground trembled somewhere behind the building, and the entire apartment groaned. Ian dove back under the covers, but the noise and movement didn't last. So, after a minute, he got out of bed and looked out the window.

In the backyard, workmen were driving twenty-foot-long metal poles into the ground at even intervals. A sandy-haired man stood at the back door, consulting a clipboard. As Ian watched, the man nodded, and blasting renewed, the workmen punching another hole into the earth.

Charlie was halfway up the stairs when he saw Grace's front door open. For weeks, every time he'd stepped into the hallway, the possibility of this moment had been at the back of his mind. Now, he felt unprepared. He hesitated, one foot dangling in the air, waiting to see her emerge.

But Grace *didn't* emerge, just a wiry guy with uncombed dark hair, and a chin covered with a few days' stubble. He wasn't wearing a shirt. The boyfriend, Charlie thought, and passed him on the landing, taking out his keys.

"Hey." Charlie turned around. The boyfriend was staring at him. "That your stuff in the yard?"

"Uh-huh," Charlie answered.

"Building something?"

"It's … an experiment."

"You a scientist?"

"A seismologist."

"No shit." The boyfriend grinned. "From Caltech?"

"CES, actually. We're a new …"

"You guys are gonna predict the Big One." The boyfriend's face opened in recognition, eyes bright as lasers. "I know you. You're the guy who predicted Kobe. I read about you in the *Reader*."

"Charlie Richter."

"Yeah, that's you." The boyfriend stepped forward and put out his hand. "My name's Ian. You want a cup of coffee?"

Ian finished brewing the last of Grace's mocha java and poured Charlie a cup. "Be honest," he said. "Is it true you guys already know how to predict earthquakes?"

Charlie laughed. He'd only known this guy five minutes, but already he was acting as if they were old friends.

"That's what they said in the *Reader*," Ian continued. "Among other things."

"Don't believe everything you read."

Charlie sipped his coffee and glanced at a stack of snapshots on the table. A pretty blonde in a bikini stood on Zuma Beach, jutting her hip provocatively and sticking out her tongue. Charlie had a pretty good idea who it was.

"That's my girlfriend," Ian said, "Grace."

Charlie examined the curve of her thigh, and the way her hair shimmered in the light. "Do you live together?"

"I have a place in Silver Lake, but Grace works all day. You work at home?"

"Sometimes. Today I'm buying a car."

"Yeah? What kind?"

"I don't know. Something simple." Charlie paused. "A Honda Civic, maybe."

"Are you kidding? Get something funky, a convertible, at least. This is L.A."

"I don't know …"

"Come on. Hondas are boring. You're not a Honda kind of guy."

Charlie looked down at the table, tracing a circle with his finger on the wood.

"Listen," Ian said. "I'll go with you. Just let me get dressed."

When he was alone, Charlie reached for the snapshots. In each, Grace stared directly into the lens, as if she knew something he would never know.

There was one Charlie couldn't get past, a close-up of her face. She wasn't smiling, and her eyes flashed with sparks that could have been excitement, or anger, or both. Charlie looked at her for a long time.

Then he heard the bedroom door open, and, almost as a reflex, he slipped the picture into his pocket. Before he could reconsider, Ian appeared.

"All right, man," he said. "Let's go buy you a car."

Grace raced home at lunch to pick up a script she'd forgotten. As usual, Navaro was sitting on the front steps.

"You're looking lovely today," he said as Grace came up the path. She smiled, but made sure not to meet his eyes.

"Hey. What's your hurry?"

"I want to say hello to Ian."

Navaro shook his head. "I don't know what you see in that guy. Hangs around here all day while you work. Doesn't even own a decent pair of pants."

Grace continued to smile.

"Anyways, he ain't up there. Took off with Charlie hours ago."

"Charlie?"

"The scientist. Went to buy a car. 'Course, I've been telling him ever since he moved in …"

But Grace was no longer listening. Charlie? With Ian? Weird. She brushed past the landlord, and went on up the stairs.

A GOOD BOSS
IS HARD TO FIND

"WHY THE FUCK DID PARAMOUNT BID ON THAT SCRIPT before we did?"

"I thought we ..."

"Don't *think*, please."

"But ..."

"This office stays on top of everything! Do you understand?"

Grace had lost the jump on Paramount. That much was true. But Ethan was *such* an asshole. He was proud of it, and *known* for it. His shirts were so starched she hoped one day his collar would slice through the tender skin of his neck. He'd bleed to death, maybe be decapitated, while the office danced around him and sang "Ding-dong, the witch is dead." Every day he trundled through those hallways, jiggling the change in his pockets, making sure his under-paid-lings did their jobs.

He'd hired Grace because he was wildly attracted to her. And not just to her sweet smile or her bouncy blonde hair. Grace was tough, and he liked tough. She was dating a screenwriter, he knew, and he'd wondered how long it would take her to bring the guy in for an assignment. It always happened, and Grace's predecessor—an unfortunate, freckled girl named Jessica—had waited only three weeks to recommend *her* lay-buddy, some dolt who wouldn't have known a plot-reversal if it slammed him in the face.

Everything Ethan had picked up at Harvard he took the wrong way. He became a prick where he might have been an authority, a cutthroat instead of a competitor, snobbish rather than stylish. He'd worked hard and done well, but even his mother didn't *like* him. Once she'd brushed the hair from his boyish face and told him she loved him. "What does that mean?" Ethan had queried. "You *have* to."

The first time he masturbated he'd used the image of his eighth-grade English teacher, Miss Templeton. But what appealed to him wasn't the deep curve of her breast underneath those silky Qiana shirts, nor her long legs, which bloomed into a perfect skirt-clad ass. No, *his* first orgasm was accompanied by the quiet repetition of what he wanted from the deal: "*A*'s and recommendations, *A*'s and recommendations ..." He derived no pleasure from the present, and had little respect for the past. After college he'd changed his name from Cohen to Carson, because he preferred how it rolled off the tongue.

Grace picked up the telephone at her desk and dialed the writer of the screenplay she had lost. She did her best to woo him to Tailspin Pictures, stating the company's successes, omitting its failures—raising her skirt verbally, so to speak. The conversation lasted only about ten minutes, but before she hung up, she'd managed to wrangle the script away from Paramount. She then called the writer's agent, a cold man with a lisp. When he found out she'd spoken directly to his client, he gave her a hard time, but Grace persisted. "I'd lay down on train tracks for this script. The fact is we *love* it. Ethan just got finished reading it and came in here, crying."

"Ethan Carson crying? Don't make me *laugh*."

But the agent came around when Grace went ahead and offered another ten thousand. As she hung up, they were even laughing about the latest O. J. Simpson joke.

She took a short stroll on the Warner lot. A feature was shooting in the soundstage around the corner, and she peeked inside a makeup trailer where she watched a young woman suddenly grow old. Grace loved movies because, like life, when you added up all the artifice, you ended up with a kind of reality. Ian could rewrite this particular script, she thought, and might not do a bad job of it. If she brought it up to Ethan at the right moment, he'd be sure to listen.

The worst thing about assholes concerns the vain hope their victims unceasingly maintain, that someday the asshole will smile. In a town of bullshitters and ass-kissers, of fair-weather fans and fly-by-night friends, only the assholes provide a true read. You expect the worst from them because the worst is the *standard*. And yet, thought Grace, once every blue moon when you do something right, what a reward it is to hear "Good job," or "Nicely done," or even "Not bad."

Such wasn't the case, today. When Grace peered into Ethan's office, and told him about her two telephone calls, her boss said to come in and close the door.

"Paramount's bid kicked out," he hissed. "Nobody wants that stupid script." Grace couldn't even muster the energy to blink. *That* explains why the writer listened so attentively, she thought, and why the agent was cordial. She decided not to tell him about the extra ten thousand.

"But, Ethan, I bought it! We *bought* it!"

There was a pause.

"Well, go back to your office, pick up the phone, and *un*buy it."

SATURDAY NIGHT

IAN DIDN'T HAVE AN AGENT EXACTLY, BUT HE DID HAVE a go-getter with a lot of energy and a car phone. Michael Lipman was his name, but sometimes he called himself "CC" (for Chutzpah-Chutzpah), and, though he had few legitimate industry concerns, the air of intrigue seemed to surround him.

When they met for the first time at his closet on Hollywood Boulevard, Michael attempted, straight away, to reach Quentin Tarantino over the speaker phone. He got as far as a personal assistant, jabbering with the woman about *Pulp* and how it saved the cinema, and what characters, what situations, what vision. What an *idiot*, Ian thought. What an exercise in humiliation. Tarantino? You don't just *call* Tarantino.

But then a man's screechy voice rose from the speaker. "Hiya, Michael," it said.

"Quentin. You don't write. You don't call." Then he sang: "You don't send me *faxes* anymore ..."

The conversation lasted a couple of minutes, during which time Ian thought how easy it is to misjudge a guy in this town. When Michael hung up, they both smiled.

Through the wall in an adjacent closet, a young man and woman, aspiring actors both, sat close together at a Salvation Army desk. They laughed heartily when the man hung up the phone, and for a moment it seemed he would kiss her full on the mouth. True, it was only voice work, but they were good mimics, and each time Michael Lipman met with a new client, he provided them with employment. Besides, he paid in cash.

Ian had sent Michael a first draft of his new screenplay, *Ear to the Ground*. And though CC hadn't read it, he did look it over for *elements*; he liked the earthquake angle, and had begun to work out a wish list of actors, including Sharon Stone and Johnny Depp. The plan was to go *wide* with it— that is, all over town. Michael was sure this would incite a bidding war. Ian had no problem with that, but he did explain he wanted *rewrite* work, and that he wasn't afraid to start at the bottom.

The following Saturday Michael called Ian at Grace's, which annoyed her a little. What annoyed her a *lot* was the agent's desperate attempt to excite Tailspin Pictures about *Ear to the Ground*. She looked away from Ian when she passed him the phone. "Get to the Café Med on Sunset, five o'clock," Michael told him.

There Ian met a skinny woman with dirty fingernails, around forty-five, who wore black, chain-smoked, and spoke Italian into a cellular phone. When he approached the table she folded up the apparatus, took his hand, and kissed both his cheeks. "I read your screenplay," she told him. "And I like very much, earthquakes."

Penniless, Ian ordered coffee. Who is this lady? Does she have any money? Michael had said she was maybe good for a treatment—a grand, tops. But as the sun set, Ian thought he might charm her into something more. A screenplay, perhaps. Things were pretty tight now; his father had finally cut him off. "Get a job," he'd said.

"But I'm a *writer*."

"And I'm a *father*, but nobody pays me for it."

It was hard for the literary artist in the twentieth century, Ian thought. Especially in this town, where screenplays came in waist-high stacks, and bus drivers along Santa Monica Boulevard pitched whole stories between Highland and La Brea. Any night of the week, if you sat at the bar at Chaya or Jones and closed your eyes, you'd hear the word *script* rolling back and forth across the room, like an auditory lava lamp. Be patient, Ian remembered, always patient. Keep the faith. In Hollywood, anything can happen.

And happen it did. After a couple of hours, a friend of the woman's arrived and she was breathtaking—a young Italian actress, quite *on fire*. She claimed she would have been the star of Fellini's last film, if Fellini had lived, but Ian didn't believe a word of it. He didn't have to, though. The waiters hovered and freshened her drinks, offering warm rolls at the flutter of an eyelash. She told a story to the skinny woman in breakneck Italian, and then, full of energy, translated it for Ian.

"I just had my fortune told by a gypsy lady."

"Uh-huh?" Ian was charmed.

"My palm." She pronounced it *PAL-lem*. "Do you know what she telled me?"

Ian shook his head.

"Destiny await you."

Then she hit the back of her hand against the table, as Italians sometimes do, and made a gap-toothed smile so stupendous that Ian had to fight the urge to grab her by the waist.

She played the saxophone, she told them, and then pulled one out of a suitcase she had lugged to the table. It was tarnished, but she sat holding it, with a reed in her mouth, smiling into Ian's eyes. Someone turned down Perry Como, and she stood up.

Sometime after midnight Ian and the actress ended up in Silver Lake, at his place. Leonetta was her name, and she blew her saxophone through the night while Ian fiddled with his trumpet. Actually, they weren't bad together. What they lacked in technical skill, they made up for with chemistry. And as they inched toward that morning hour where spending the night becomes a foregone conclusion, Ian noticed the light blinking like crazy on his answering machine, while he played an unpleasant, abstract riff, and considered how to go about suggesting the sleeping arrangements.

SATURDAY NIGHT, PART TWO

GRACE WAS PISSED. IAN'S RIDICULOUS AGENT HAD CALLED and harassed her—at home, for Christ's sake—about *Ear to the Ground*. What a joker Michael Lipman was. Here it was, Saturday night, and he had set up some kind of meeting. Grace was so angry she hardly even looked up when Ian headed for the door. "I'll call you," he told her.

Three hours later, though, Ian still hadn't called, and Grace had moved toward the numb realization that she'd been taken for granted again. It was almost summer, and the days were languid, nearly tropical. As twilight settled over the city and fog began to drift across the Hollywood Hills, Grace found herself pacing the rooms of her apartment, imagining a man who wouldn't leave her hanging on a Saturday, who would maybe buy her flowers once in a while, clean up the kitchen after himself, or at least replace the coffee when he'd used it up.

She dialed Ian's number, left a nasty message, and went to get her keys. Fuck him, she thought. She didn't need Ian. She was an adult. She could take care of herself. There was that new place on Beverly they'd been wanting to try, where she could get a nice piece of fish, lightly grilled, and a glass of wine. And after that … well, she could always read a couple of scripts.

Navaro was on the building's front stoop when Grace reached the bottom of the stairs. Please don't talk to me, she thought, and then: I don't have to deal with you, I can just go on my way. But he said hello and, of course, she said hi, cursing herself for not having the strength to be rude.

"All alone tonight?" Navaro asked. In her faded jeans and T-shirt, Grace clearly was not dressed for a date.

"Ian's working."

"He don't know the meaning of the word." Navaro shook his head with a bitter little laugh. "He sits around all day and works on Saturday *night*? The whole time me and Elise, God forgive her, were together, I'd always be home by six-thirty, every Saturday night."

God forgive her? Grace thought. "That's nice," she said.

"Yeah. Elise." Over Navaro's shoulder, the last dregs of daylight faded to black. "I ever show you her picture?"

"No." Grace's stomach tightened like a fist.

"Wanna see?"

She hesitated, and Navaro took that for a yes. He headed for his front door, leaving her on the steps to wait for him.

Just then, a Honda Civic pulled up in front of the building, and Charlie climbed out the passenger side. He leaned into the open window and looked at Kenwood, who was sitting in the driver's seat, hands tight on the wheel.

"You're not gonna go home and stare at her picture, are you?" Charlie asked.

Kenwood shook his head.

"You want to get some dinner?"

"Not hungry."

"Then do me one favor? Don't go jumping off any bridges."

"What bridge did you have in mind?" Kenwood looked up.

"Good point." Charlie smiled, and backed away from the car. "So I'll see you Monday?"

Kenwood nodded, and the Civic crawled away from the curb.

Grace watched the sandy-haired man walk up the path, flickering in and out of patches of lamplight.

"You must be Charlie," she said.

"And you must be Grace."

They smiled for a moment that stretched nearly into discomfort. Then Navaro's door squeaked open, and Grace's face fell like a stone.

"Do you know about computers and everything?" She spoke quickly, moving her face toward Charlie's ear.

Charlie didn't understand.

"I mean, you work with them, don't you?"

"Yeah ..."

Before Grace could elaborate, Navaro came up behind them, bearing a photograph of a middle-aged woman in a ratty bouffant. "I see you two met," he said, wheezing a little, a Pall Mall hanging from his lips.

"Incorrect path, incorrect path," Grace said to Charlie. "Every time I try it, I keep getting 'incorrect path.'" Her eyes sparkled, and a smile crept from the corners of her mouth. "I'm so confused."

Briefly, the three of them stood in suspension, and even the crickets in the cool Los Angeles night seemed to grow still.

"Probably have to defrag the system," Charlie told her. "Right away."

"You guys with your computers," Navaro laughed, shaking his head. And as quickly as he had appeared, he was gone.

"Thanks," Grace said to Charlie when they reached the second floor landing.

"No problem." He turned slightly toward his door. Something in his way reminded Grace of an old boyfriend who'd never taken the initiative, always waiting for her to make the first move. Charlie would be like that, she figured. But it didn't matter, she was with Ian, and Ian ...

... was nowhere to be found.

"Hey." Grace made sure to keep her voice neutral. "What are you doing right now?"

"Nothing."

"You hungry?"

"I am, actually." He patted his stomach. "But I have work to do."

"Me too, but you gotta eat."

"That's true."

"We could order Chinese."

Charlie nodded. "I like Chinese."

"Great," Grace said. "Why don't I go dig up a menu, and I'll knock on your door?"

In her apartment Grace grabbed the bottle of good red she'd been saving, dialed Ian's number, and was happy to get his machine. On her way out, she looked at the pile of scripts, and wondered about falling behind. But once she stepped onto the landing, and approached Charlie's door, work was the last thing on her mind.

PRIMARY DISTURBANCE FORCES

IF YOU LOOKED AT A MAP, YOU'D THINK NORTH AMERICA began at the Atlantic shore and ran west to the Pacific— through that wide, misunderstood state of Ohio, across forgettable Indiana and the confounding yellow-green flatness of Kansas and eastern Colorado. Suddenly, there are the Rockies, whose remotest peaks and crags were never touched by man or woman.

Past those mountains, to the southwest, lonely desert winds swirl among the Mojave's dunes and bring dust to the blacktops and souvenir stands, whirring by the gilded death they call Las Vegas, and carrying a whore's cheap perfume to the California border. The bleakness is broken by San Bernardino; and beyond, at the edge of the continent, lies the great salty municipality of Santa Monica. There you go—from coa to shining sea. But here's the catch: The earth has only *one* continent, *one* floor, *one* ground. We live on an assemblage of tectonic plates, joined casually, sometimes grinding, and always sliding underneath us. Perhaps this is what we mean when we speak of the connectedness of all things.

Charlie had been startled. Leaning against a mound of dirt precisely at position D-55 of the San Andreas Fault, and wiping from his hand some mayonnaise from a chicken sandwich, he was working out a simple algorithm. Then suddenly, in the thick of his data, he came upon a curious block of prime numbers—which wasn't alarming per se, but their proliferation did give him pause, which, in turn, brought him focus. Prime numbers were strange: divisible only by themselves and by the number one, they were anomalies, set off, unrelated. They reminded Charlie of a young boy poring over his butterflies while the other kids were out playing in the street. And here was a veritable *convention* of butterfly collectors, a group of misfit integers, crying for attention.

After looking at the numbers some more, he took a long swig of water and recapped his bottle, thinking. Fault lines may be important, but *plate tectonic*s were the Primary Disturbance Forces in the area. And Charlie understood plates. In the mid-1980s a man named Locksley had made brave statements about them, and had been run out of American seismology on a rail. But Locksley had missed an integral piece of the puzzle, and in his passion for plates he'd overlooked fault lines entirely.

Fault lines were important, Charlie knew, but only as *conductors* of the disturbances caused by the slippage of plates—not vice versa. This was where the Caltechies had gone wrong; it explained why they'd never predicted an earthquake, and why, Charlie thought with a smirk, they'd never offered him a job. At that moment he felt relieved by the simplicity of his task: to locate which plates were slipping, and wait. This much he'd been doing for more than a year. All that was missing was the link between the plates and these prime numbers. He knew, and yet he didn't know.

He studied the data a while longer, and his heart beat with increased fervor. He packed up his gear, crammed it into the minuscule trunk of his forest green Miata, and shook his head. (The dealer had told him it was big enough to hold a set of golf clubs. He hadn't considered the *bag*.) As the sun began to set, Charlie drove through the desert with the top down, thinking how some would consider the view romantic. Yet, twisting and turning beneath purple skies, he felt suddenly alone.

In the chairman's office at the Center for Earthquake Studies, Sterling Caruthers sat behind his desk in a high-back leather chair, swiveling left and right in jerky movements, and consulting a calendar. Today was the twenty-third of June, he noticed, and sometime before the end of the year, he vowed, his organization would predict a major earthquake. His boys were close. That Kenwood—morose as he was—could program a computer to buy a beer and piss for you; and then there was Charlie Richter. The wild card. Caruthers didn't like the guy but he knew he was a brilliant scientist, and wondered how long before Richter would do in L.A. what he'd done in Kobe.

Not that Caruthers particularly gave a shit about science; it might as well have been stocks and bonds, or real estate. But he'd found another land of opportunity—the land of *earthquakes*. Leaning back, he considered the advantages of knowing when and where a quake would hit. The possibilities were endless. He smiled, glanced at his hairy knuckles, and—stretching fingertips *up*—examined his nails. Then he unzipped a small leather case, extracted some silver-plated tools, and began to give himself a manicure.

THE NUMBERS GAME

CHARLIE'S EYES SNAPPED OPEN IN THE DARKNESS LIKE window shades. The digital clock screamed out the time in bright broken red. Twelve twenty-nine. One, two, twenty-nine. Prime numbers again. Maybe if he just closed his eyes, everything would be there, waiting for him. But when he tried, there were only grainy little patches of black.

Damn, he thought. He was so close; he could feel the connections struggling to be made. It was like the slow slipping of tectonic plates as they made their inevitable journeys apart. That was still what captivated Charlie most about seismology: the way the earth seemed so solid on the surface, yet was in a constant state of flux. Just the other day, walking from his Miata to the Versateller machine near the La Brea Tar Pits, he'd looked at the tall buildings lining Wilshire Boulevard, and thought how illusory they were, monuments to stability on a planet where the only constant was change. They were like prayers, these buildings, like gestures of faith in some kind of permanence that no one really believed, but which they counted on just the same. This was the bedrock principle all Angelenos shared, the hope that the city would hold together, and life on the fault line could be more than an extended waiting game.

Charlie got out of bed and walked naked through his darkened apartment. Something in his mind flashed like a strobe, the hall and the interior stairway appearing in flickers of shadow and light. Downstairs, he glanced towards the corner, where a seismograph traced a line so straight the earth itself appeared dead. Then, he sat at his computer console and listened to the humming of the machines, which gave him a delicious tickle in the pit of his stomach and along the surface of his scrotum.

"Okay," he said to himself, barely aware that he had spoken. "Let's see what we have." He tapped a key, and two parallel columns of numbers scrolled across the screen. On another console, he accessed CES, and brought up a map of the western United States. He punched in a few coordinates, and a handful of red markers appeared.

Charlie heard the window rattle, and reached out to steady himself. Was that another one? Ever since Sunday night, when he'd been awakened by a cluster of temblors—a 4.9 and a couple of mid-3s—Charlie had been waiting. Publicly, he'd gone along with the idea that these were just aftershocks, but inside, he knew they were something more. Aftershocks were a fiction, a myth to soothe the worries of non-scientific minds. Earthquakes were connected, that much was true, but the connections were bigger than anyone at CalTech, or CES for that matter, was willing to admit. Charlie looked over at the seismograph. The needle remained still, but he couldn't shake the feeling that something had happened, or was about to happen. Without thinking, he got up and headed for the back door.

Ian was reading next to a sleeping Grace when he heard the squeak of door springs downstairs. Quietly, gently, so as not to disturb her, he eased his naked body off the bed and crept to the window. For a moment, it was difficult to see the yard. Then, Ian made out a figure bent over the base of one of those metal poles. Charlie, he thought, and looked at the clock. It was one twenty-three. How weird.

But things got even weirder when Charlie stood up and caught the light. He was naked, too, crossing the yard without a stitch of clothing. Ian thought about waking Grace, but immediately decided against it. Instead, he dropped into a crouch by the window, and watched his neighbor make his way among the poles like a celebrant in some arcane religious rite.

Charlie was unsettled just then. There was still something he was missing, some information his machines couldn't provide. He considered going back to the numbers, but he knew they weren't enough.

All of a sudden it came to him. The soil samples. He had collected dirt from seven local faults, and the analysis reports were sitting in the Prediction Lab. It might be late, but he'd never fall back asleep, so he went inside, threw on some clothes, and zoomed off to CES.

The Center for Earthquake Studies was hulking and dark, and Charlie moved through it like a ghost. In the Prediction Lab, he began to pore over the soil analysis charts, checking them against the wall map.

For more than an hour, Charlie struggled to make sense of the numbers swimming before his eyes. Then he got up, and sat in the corner by the door. With some difficulty, he assumed the lotus position and, concentrating on the steady pattern of his breathing, emptied his mind until there was nothing left within him but light.

When Charlie returned to his computer, he saw it instantly. A group of samples, abnormally high in alkaline, were clustered in an area near the epicenter of the Northridge quake. He converted their parameters into numbers, and each one came up prime.

In a daze, Charlie went to the phone, dialed half of Kenwood's number, and stopped. It's three seventeen, he thought. Besides, none of this means anything yet. There's work to do. He turned to his screen and looked back at the numbers. He was still looking at them six hours later, when Kenwood got to work.

INDEPENDENCE DAY

CHARLIE WAS FINGERING THE HOLES ON THE SLENDER wooden neck of a recorder when he heard a knock at his back door. Some kids learned baseball from their dads, some learned chess, some learned how to make their ways in the world. Charlie had learned only a love of music from his father. Although he'd wished for more from the old man, at least, he thought, this was something.

Grace waited on the landing, sagging under the weight of a case of beer and three bags of store-bought ice. When Charlie opened the door, her face lit up.

"Happy Fourth," she said. "Still OK to keep this in your fridge?"

"Uh, sure." He made no effort to get out of the way.

"You gonna let me in?"

"Sorry." Charlie passed a hand across his face.

"I didn't know you were a musician." Grace nodded at the recorder, which dangled from his hand. She slipped around him into his kitchen, their arms touching as she passed.

"I just like to mess around."

"Ian has the same problem." Grace's voice was flat as sand. "Of course, his weakness is the trumpet." She slid bottles of beer into the refrigerator's empty maw. "He used to play for me, but he doesn't anymore." Looking up, she flashed another smile. "You could, though."

For a moment, Charlie stood there, hands useless as fishhooks. Then he raised the recorder to his lips and began an Elizabethan madrigal, notes hanging in the air like questions.

Ian was stoking briquets when he heard a high, thin melody coming from Charlie's apartment. People would be here any minute, and Grace was getting some kind of private *concert*, for Christ's sake. This party was her idea; he had gone along only because she'd been strange lately. Ever since that night with Leonetta. He shrugged the thought away like a nettlesome insect, but not before wondering if there was any way she could *know*.

"Grace?" He turned the coals with a set of tongs to make sure they were red. "Grace!"

The only response was an old-fashioned twist of music that made him think of Leonetta's French braid.

Ian trudged across the backyard to Charlie's door. He knocked once, and the playing stopped. Seconds later, Charlie appeared, lips swollen as if from a long kiss.

"Ian," Charlie said.

Grace leaned against the refrigerator, cheeks lightly flushed. Her eyes sparkled.

"How's it going?" she asked, unable to meet Ian's gaze. Briefly, she had a vision of herself thirty years in the future, sitting with Charlie on a blue velour couch surrounded by photographs and other mementos. She could feel the fuzzy texture of the upholstery, and his body pressing against hers. When she attempted to conjure the same image with Ian, she couldn't see beyond where they were right then.

"Hate to disturb you," Ian said, "but what about the chairs?"

"Oh, right." Grace's voice fluttered like a hummingbird, unsure where to land. "Sorry. We were just ..." She trailed off, and headed for the door.

"Need help?" Charlie asked, watching her from behind.

Grace turned. "We're OK, I think. But you're coming, right? You said you would."

Charlie nodded.

"Good," Grace said.

Ian watched Grace set a hodgepodge of chairs around the backyard, placing them away from the network of poles. If he didn't know better, he'd think something had happened in Charlie's kitchen, but Charlie wasn't Grace's type. Grace liked a bit of wildness that Charlie didn't have; she had always been attracted by Ian's disheveled good looks, his rumpled pants and torn sweaters. Anyway, there was a big difference between a trumpet and a recorder, and Grace was definitely a trumpeter's woman. I'm just being paranoid, Ian thought, and walked across the lawn, wrapping his arms around Grace's waist from behind.

A month ago, or even less, Grace would have tilted her head back so Ian could nuzzle her neck, maybe even moving her butt against him in a gesture somewhere between a grind and a caress. But today, she did neither. She stood rigid for a moment, waiting, it seemed, until he was finished. Then she wriggled free and took a couple of steps away. When Ian came closer, she turned and stopped him with her hand.

"Not now," she said.

"What?"

"People are coming."

"You could be one of them."

"I could be a lot of things."

"What do you mean by that?"

"You know what I mean."

Later, the backyard was filled with people, and music from a boom box drifted through the flat summer air. Grace checked the cooler and found the beer supply had dwindled, so she went into Charlie's apartment to retrieve the bottles she had stored there.

It was cool and dark inside. Grace paused at the refrigerator, then turned and passed through the door into Charlie's computer room. She trailed her fingers along the edge of a table, and noticed the seismograph etching straight and silent lines. Sitting next to it was Charlie's recorder. Grace picked it up, letting her fingers fall across the holes. Without thinking, she raised the instrument to her lips and gave a tentative blow. A reedy chirp broke the stillness, and Grace jumped a little. She lingered at the table, the trace of a smile dancing on and off her face, and wondered where things could possibly go from here.

THE WAY OF ZEN

I'LL STAY IN BED, IAN THOUGHT, AS HE PULLED A RATTY down comforter over his chest and splayed his arms outside it. He hadn't had gas at his Silver Lake apartment since the brown uniformed man left a disconnection notice and disapeared down the garden path. Who needs gas? Ian looked at a crack in the ceiling. For that matter, who needs *electricity*?

He closed his eyes, but his brain was too active for sleeping. Behind his lids came an image of a tower of bills he had constructed, next to the phone, over a six-month period. If debtors' prison still existed, he'd be in chains. His car—a metazoan BMW—was a piece of shit, but had once been a *running* piece of shit. Having lost respect for its driver, it now started less than 20 percent of the time. Ian once felt elegant behind the wheel of that classic luxury sedan—but now he felt like fallen aristocracy, shammed by Hollywood and awakened from the American Dream.

He opened his eyes, threw off the covers, and brought his feet to the floor. I could get a *job*, he thought for less than a second, and then summoned his "girls," as he referred to the pile of pornography he kept on the floor of his closet: several *Penthouse* magazines purchased incognito at a newsstand, along with a slew of Victoria's Secret catalogs filched from the mail box of the woman upstairs. Masturbation may be dirty, he thought, and its pleasures fleeting—but at least it was truly *free*.

Which was more than you could say for a lot of things. Like relationships. Or friendships. Nothing beats a social connection, Ian thought, and you never forget a guy once you smoke a joint with him in some parking lot. The Formosa on Thursday nights yielded *mucho connectiones industrio*. Sometimes he'd even move the crowd over to Bar Deluxe, where he played his horn with Raf Green's band. But it all had its price.

Ten minutes later, Ian lay in a sea of Kleenex, wondering lazily what it took for a writer to get work in Los Angeles. Then he stood under a hot but under-pressured shower. He dragged the soap across his genitals. Why did he always do that first? Not a bad character thing. I'll use it, he thought.

Refreshed, Ian left a message on Michael Lipman's staticky answering machine and thought about how to find another agent. Last month Michael had told him things were *heating up* with the script, that buyers were circling like hawks and it was only a matter of time. But who was he kidding? *Ear to the Ground* was dead. Prospects were flatter than a Paris crêpe. As he booted his computer to work on the screenplay some more, he forced himself to think about what would really *happen* to Los Angeles if Caltech or CES predicted an earthquake? He scrolled to the big scene on page seventy-five. Los Angeles gets plunged into turmoil around page forty (Syd Field would be proud), and the city spends much of act two breaking apart in anticipation of the Big One (a nifty piece of irony, he thought smugly). I'll knock heads a little more with my main character, he thought. If I got to *know* him better, who knows?

Ian was struck by how easily he wrote good supporting characters, yet at the same time, left his protagonist a gaping vortex. Why does everything happen *to* him? What does he *do*? Then again, what does *anybody* do? What do *agents* do? They certainly don't call a guy back. Agents are persistent by profession, Ian thought. But in Hollywood, the chain of desperation has many links. Even Mike Ovitz gets blown off sometimes.

Never take things personally. Always be detached. Ian had heard that Ovitz had studied Buddhism in college. So, from his bookcase, he extracted Alan Watts's *The Way of Zen* and read the first five pages of the introduction.

Satisfied with the completeness of his study, he walked over to the window and opened the blinds. The sun was hot and bright and critical, and it occurred to him then that he wouldn't be able to pay his rent even if he found a job. He had two days to rescue his phone. An auto-registration-due notice was propped against his computer monitor, next to some parking tickets, which he sometimes used as bookmarks. And he *did* need electricity. He had lied to his creditors about having already sold *Ear to the Ground*. The price, he'd told them, was in the high six figures, but studio business affairs were slow-moving. At first, the collection agents had been friendly, even congratulatory. But they're not idiots. Once they found out the truth, he'd never get any credit for the rest of his life. Ian sat there, having nothing, owing everything, and for a long time he didn't move. Then he yanked a cord, and the dusty blinds went down with a crack. What a delightful image, Ian thought, for my biographers.

 SHAKING ALL OVER

CHARLIE WAS HEADING OUT TO THE FIELD. IT WAS TEN o'clock on a Thursday evening, and he was in the kitchen, preparing a Thermos of coffee for the night ahead. Ever since he'd deciphered those prime numbers, he'd been running computer simulations of local faults, and if his data was right, there would be a small earthquake along the San Andreas sometime before dawn. It was a long shot, he knew, but he had to see.

Charlie packed the coffee in a rucksack, then loaded his laptop and a couple of empty sample trays. He thought again about the numbers, the alkalinity of the soil. The Northridge data had been the first indicator, but when he'd gone back and looked at the information from Indio, he'd begun to understand that this was bigger than he'd thought. He remembered the day his grandfather had explained how fault lines were interrelated. "Think of the faults as highways," the old man had said, "and earthquakes as cars. Some cars remain on one road, but others take exits and branch off. It's the same with temblors. Conceivably, a big enough jolt could trigger any number of quakes up and down the line."

Indeed, Charlie thought. Up and down the line. He shouldered the rucksack and moved toward the door.

Outside, Charlie ran into Ian coming up the path. Ian looked more disheveled than usual, with big black circles under his eyes.

"Hey," Charlie said. "How you doing? Haven't seen you around."

"Everything's fucked." Ian put his hands in his pockets and attempted a grin. His face looked hollow, like a lost little boy's. "Grace up there?" He nodded toward her apartment.

"Couldn't tell you."

"Yeah, well …" He stared at her windows for a moment, then focused on Charlie's rucksack. "Where *you* off to?"

"Duty calls."

"A seismologist's work is never done?"

"Something like that. Earthquakes are unpredictable."

"So they say." Ian threw him a sly grin. "You want company? I'm dying to see what you do."

"Maybe some other time," Charlie said. "The desert's no place…"

"The *desert*?" Ian's eyes lit up like fluorescent bulbs. "You going to the San Andreas?"

"Yeah," Charlie said. "There's something there I have to do."

Charlie took the 10 to San Bernardino, his Miata cutting like a laser through the night. Just east of the city, he turned north off the freeway, then went east again to position D-55 of the San Andreas Fault.

The desert night was cool and still, and Charlie uncorked his Thermos of coffee immediately. Sipping slowly, he walked around the perimeter of the site. Here, the San Andreas cut a visible rift through the brown rocky earth; it looked like a furrow, made by some gigantic plow. He sat on one raised edge of the fault line and turned his face to the sky.

Charlie loved the desert at night. The sky was filled with clustered stars, dotting the blackness in pinpricks of light. Sitting with his coffee, Charlie began to name the constellations—Big Dipper, Little Dipper, and the three sharp points of Orion's Belt. If he listened closely to the silence, he could almost hear his father, the astronomer, dismissing his grandfather's work. "Long after the planet has disappeared into the sun," Charlie's father liked to say, "the stars will continue to exist. Of what importance will earthquakes be then?" In a way, Charlie knew, he was right, but there had always been a coldness to the heavens that could not compete with the warmth of the world, the way a stone kept its heat long after the sun had set. The stars were distant, beautiful like diamonds, but unfeeling, abstract. Thinking about it, Charlie realized his father was much the same way, which, he suddenly understood, explained a lot.

Charlie removed a sample tray from his rucksack and slipped down into the fault. As he scraped some dirt from the bottom of the fissure, the earthquake struck. At first, there was a low rumbling, like the sound of an oncoming train, then the ground started twisting in a side-to-side motion, and the walls of the San Andreas shook like something from a bad horror film. Charlie tried to stand, but was thrown to his knees. Reflexively, he put his hands out, one on either edge of the fault. The vibrations moved from the earth through his palms, and up his arms to his heart.

When the temblor was over, Charlie lay in the fault fissure and drew a deep breath. His whole body rang from the shaking; his legs were weak and spent. He tried to catalog what had happened. Intense as it seemed, this had been a small earthquake, probably no larger than a 4.5. The jolt couldn't have lasted more than a couple of seconds, but from where Charlie sat, the world felt upside down. I just rode out a quake from the center of the San Andreas, he thought, but his mind wouldn't grasp the particulars, and it was all he could do to scramble up the side of the ridge. Although it didn't look like there'd been any substantial slippage, he scooped up some additional soil samples to bring to CES.

Back at the car, Charlie retrieved his laptop and ran the simulation program, extending the parameters to see what might happen next. The San Andreas was becoming increasingly active—he'd known that since Indio—but without the exact epicenter of this event, it was impossible to tell what anything meant. He needed more information, to see what the numbers looked like now. Charlie loaded up his rucksack and started on the long ride home.

RECOMMENDATION: PASS

DRIPPING PICTURES
Title: Ear to the Ground
Writer: Ian Marcus

Analyst: Belladonna
7/28/95

Type of Material: SP
118 pp.
Dated. 6/16/95

		exclt	good	fair	poor
Elements: Johnny Depp (?)					
Sub by: ML	Premise			X	
Sub to: EH	Story Line			X	
Genre: Disaster Drama	Structure		X		
Time: Present	Characterization			X	
Location: Southern California	Dialogue		X		

Recommendation: Pass
Writer: Maybe

Log Line: A journalist, unable to sleep for fear of earthquakes, finds out the Big One is coming to Los Angeles and that seismologists know about it. What they don't know is how to alert the city without plunging the populace into turmoil.

Comment Summary: This story alternates between gentle earnestness and biting sarcasm. *Earthquake* meets *Network*. There's more science than there needs to be, and I'm not sure audiences will buy the paranoid theory behind it.

Synopsis: BILL MARTIN is a razor-stubbled reporter at the *Los Angeles Sun*. He's frequently at odds with his editor,

GERARD CONSINO, a small, wiry man with little vision. Bill can't sleep nights, what with recurring nightmares of the earth opening up and swallowing his Silver Lake apartment building whole. At an editorial meeting one morning, he proposes the idea that earthquakes can be predicted, but the techies are holding out. "Another one of your conspiracy theories?" Gerard asks him.

This angers Bill. He imagines his colleagues talking behind his back and begins to worry that the slightest vibration—a refrigerator's hum or the passing of a bus—is an earthquake. His bad dreams become more frequent, and one night he is compelled to walk through the streets of Los Angeles. He has never done this before, and he finds the sensation thrilling. At 3 a.m., he lies down in the middle of Wilshire Boulevard and puts his ear to the ground. Underneath him is a fault line, and he hears a rumbling from the center of the earth, which he understands like a language. (*Doctor Doolittle*?) The cops pick him up and keep him briefly under observation.

A few nights later, while roaming the Hollywood Hills, Bill encounters two seismologists discussing a field experiment they're conducting in a canyon. One of them keeps saying, "My God, I don't believe it." The other says, "Relax." They've predicted the Big One.

The seismologists find it uncanny that Bill understands the ins and outs of earthquake prediction. They tell him about their experiments, describing how their soil samples yielded an abnormally high alkaline content, and how it was possible to predict patterns once they considered all the factors involved. (Science gets a little thin here.)

Bill becomes the seismologists' shadow, following their experiments as best he can. Eventually, the data points in one direction: In exactly five months and five days, at five minutes after five in the morning, an earthquake of between 8.9 and 9.1 will hit near San Bernardino.

Bill writes up the story and turns in a preliminary draft, stressing that it shouldn't be printed until an agreement can be reached about how best to inform the public. But Gerard publishes the story immediately.

Los Angeles is understandably shocked. People talk (seriously) about leaving. The real estate market bottoms out. Religious fanatics take their prayers to the street corners. Each day, dogs bark more loudly.

The *Sun* is catapulted to fame, and Bill is nominated for a Pulitzer. But his work suffers. He stops bathing and becomes uninterested in sex. When he begins to live like an animal, his girl friend leaves him. He goes into the hills, burrowing with the coyotes and living off nuts and berries.

As droves of Angelenos leave the city, the mayor announces that the whole thing is a hoax. The populace is divided between believers and skeptics. Earthquake drills become commonplace in schools. The Dodgers move back to Brooklyn.

The clock is ticking. When summer passes into fall, and winter's rains begin, Bill decides to lead the remaining citizens away from L.A. Like Christ, or the Pied Piper, he summons them on the eve of the earthquake, and they follow him north. Riding in his car is SHEILA, the beautiful wife of one of the original seismologists—although her husband has stayed behind to observe the quake.

Right on schedule, the earth shakes. Buildings tumble. Hollywood is completely destroyed. Burbank is busted, and Venice goes up in flames. Century Park East collapses onto Avenue of the Stars.

In San Luis Obispo, Bill takes the news hard. Half the remaining populace is thought to be dead. Bill and his group make their way south to do what they can, but with the freeways destroyed, travel is slow. Eventually, they arrive on foot and contribute to the rescue effort.

While ABC looks for Bill, hoping to put him on *Nightline*, he is off with Sheila, searching for her husband. They find him just as he utters his dying words: "Take good care of my wife."

Bill and Sheila bury the seismologist by the beach and walk quietly as the waves lap at their feet. They kiss.

Comments: This kind of sensationalist trash preys on human fear and paranoia. As such, it could become a blockbuster. Still, the writing is uneven; the writer unproven. I'd make the protagonist a seismologist, not a journalist. The reporter should be the corrupt one. Johnny Depp passed, as did directors Andrew Davis, James Cameron, and Wolfgang Petersen.

Although there hasn't been a really good natural disaster picture in two decades, people have already pretty much forgotten about Northridge. With the ground silent and still, this just isn't topical.

PASS.

 HITTING THE FAN

"LISTEN," IAN WAS SAYING, "I DON'T MEAN TO BE PUSHY ..."

"But?"

"Come on, Grace. You know what I mean."

Ian glared across the table. It was late Sunday morning, and he was sitting with Grace on the sidewalk outside Quality, traffic racing past on Third Street as they waited for their food. Inside the restaurant, Ian could see Elliott Gould and, slouched over coffee and toast at another table, Drew Barrymore and Eric Erlandson. Ah, Hollywood, where celebrity was a spectator sport, and just going out for brunch was like being on TV.

Ian ran a hand across his face. Two tables away, a redheaded woman and a guy with a gray ponytail sat facing a stroller, chattering at a brown-haired baby with two tiny teeth. All of a sudden, the kid caught Ian's eye and grinned. Ian tried to imagine what it would be like to be so young, so open to the world. Then he looked up, and Grace gave him such a tired stare he felt he'd never be young again.

"What?" he asked her.

"It's not my fault your life's falling apart."

"My life's *not* falling apart."

"Whatever you say."

"It's a good script, Grace."

"That's not the point."

"That's the *whole* point."

"Tracy lost her job going out on that limb."

"You're not going out on any *limb*." Ian leaned across the table and smiled. "Trust me."

"You keep saying that."

Charlie was on his way out when he heard voices in the hall. He waited until the noise receded before he emerged into the white summer heat. These last few days, he'd felt a little off, as if the unsteady earth were transferring some of its shakiness to the marrow of his bones, leaving him unsure how to behave. Now that the entryway was deserted, he breathed a silent prayer of thanks.

No sooner had Charlie stepped outside than he heard someone call his name from above. On the second-floor landing, Ian stood at the rail.

"Hey." Ian waved. "You got a minute?"

Charlie nodded.

"I wanna ask you something."

A shape flickered behind Ian like a ghost. At first, Charlie thought it was a shadow, but then he noticed a sweep of blonde hair, and recognized Grace. Her lips were pinched white. They've been fighting, Charlie thought, and for some reason, this gave him a jolt of glee.

"The other night?" Ian leaned closer. "When you went to the desert?"

Charlie nodded again.

"You knew it was coming, didn't you?"

Grace stepped out of the shadows. "Jesus, Ian. Give it a rest."

"Tell me the truth," Ian continued.

"Maybe a hunch," Charlie said.

Ian broke into a toothy grin and turned to Grace. "You see? Now you gonna give it to Ethan?"

"You don't give up, do you?" Grace hissed. She glared at Ian for a second, then stormed away, footsteps like gunshots from inside.

Half an hour later, Charlie drove down Culver Boulevard, trying to clear his head. He had wanted today to be quiet; he had wanted to look at numbers, at the newest projections of activity on the Pacific Plate. That was what the San Andreas was telling him: Kobe's shocks were moving east.

The Center for Earthquake Studies was empty, sunlight falling in dusty shafts across the floor. In the lab, Charlie checked the wall map out of habit and looked again for a pattern in the pushpins. An hour later, he had reduced a sixty-four-bit matrix to a sixteen-bit matrix but had learned nothing.

Charlie was in the middle of an elaborate simulation program when he heard a noise from beyond the door. He waited, head cocked like a hunting dog's. A softer sound came, and Charlie left his computer and went to investigate.

At first, Charlie didn't notice anything unusual. Then he saw that the door to Caruthers's office was open, and he caught a glimpse of an unfurled sleeping bag on the couch. In the room, a backpack lay half empty on the floor. Charlie was about to examine its contents when he heard a cough and turned to find Kenwood standing in the door.

"What's going on?" Charlie said. "Are you … ?"

"I can't go home. I get in the car, and I can't go home. I just sit there. Since Tuesday."

"You've been here since Tuesday?"

"It's the only place I feel safe."

Kenwood rocked back and forth in the doorway, as if doing some kind of dance.

"Have you been looking at her picture?" Charlie asked.

"No. But I'm scared."

"Scared of what?"

"It's just this feeling I have." Kenwood leaned against the doorjamb and took a long breath. "Everything's about to hit the fan."

SAN ANDREAS, D-55–
8.9–DECEMBER 29, 1995

ACTORS SAY THEY FEEL AT HOME IN A THEATER, ANY theater, anywhere. Chefs love kitchens, and taxi drivers live for green lights strung to the horizon. But Charlie Richter loved numbers. He lived with them, found meaning in them. Like a jigsaw puzzle, he could fit the pieces together by applying correct persistence.

Charlie printed hard copies of his numerical tables after the computer monitor began to make his eyes twitch. He lay on the Prediction Lab floor, the carpet digging into his elbows, looking at numbers. Eight-digit prime numbers, nine-digit prime numbers, ten-digit ones. He was tired, and had been considering taking a nap on the floor when he saw it. The number first appeared at the beginning of his tables, and popped up again nearly thirty pages later. A layman would never have recognized the repeated value because he would have ascribed no meaning to it. But Charlie noticed that the two numbers, expressed logarithmically, were identical—the way a guitarist finds different ways to play the same chord.

The double incidence was nothing in itself, Charlie knew, but when he applied this particular integer as a static coefficient, he arrived at a value equidistant from the perimetary, or "bookend," members of the matrix. Charlie was suddenly able to ascertain the epicenter of a major seismic event. He felt flush then, and began to sweat. Soon the massive logarithm was entirely solvable, like a crossword puzzle, when one nagging four-letter word leads to ten others: Moments after he'd locked down the epicenter (E), Charlie had solved for the quake's occurrence date (OD) and magnitude (M).

Months and months of struggle and discontinuity came together in a matter of seconds. He had suspected a sizable earthquake was coming, but now he knew *exactly* what to expect. He took a deep breath and looked over at the map of Southern California. Then, on the back of a tattered envelope, he wrote carefully:

San Andreas, D-55 8.9 December 29th, 1995

Sterling Caruthers arrived at the Center for Earthquake Studies and went to his office to pick up some e-mail from his newest mistress. When he found none, he got up and ambled through the empty building, having learned to stay atop of his underlings by rifling through their drawers at night. Much to his surprise, he discovered Charlie Richter still tinkering away at this late hour. Noticing the envelope propped against Charlie's monitor, he picked it up, and looked at it closely. "What's this?" Caruthers wanted to know.

"Sterling, I ... "

It dawned on him. "Eight-point-nine?! My *God!*" Caruthers was suddenly buoyant.

"Listen," Charlie implored, "before we do anything, I need to double-check every single value in this enormous matrix. That'll take time, okay?"

"How much time?"

"A week, at least. Maybe ten days ..."

"Of course," Sterling said gently.

"Thank you," Charlie said.

There was a pause. Charlie hadn't expected Caruthers to be so understanding, and it disarmed him. "I'm scared," Charlie blurted out. "I don't know what's worse: the quake, or what's gonna happen ..." He didn't finish. He meant, of course, what might happen after the announcement was made. When the people found out, and panicked. When they considered that the city they'd been building on the edges of mountainsides would tumble into the sea.

When we're slow and our minds are slow, we wallow in a pool of time, and tread the stagnant water. I am a lily, Ian thought, browning at the edges. What about law school? There's still time. Thirty-one isn't *old*. He closed his eyes with disgust, and decided he would trade his life for virtually anyone's. Then he felt almost cheerful, having lost all hope, because hope was the drug that had driven him down. Ian picked up Alan Watts's *The Way of Zen* and flung it across the room.

An hour later he lay in bed, alone in his Silver Lake apartment, but he couldn't fall asleep. He picked up the phone, woke his parents in Philadelphia, and told his father he'd decided to go to law school. The sleepy response was: "We'll talk tomorrow." Ian came to the sad conclusion that he couldn't confide in anyone about the sorry state of his life. To call a friend in the industry would be admitting defeat. By morning it would be all over town that Ian Marcus's career was in the toilet. *What* career? he thought. Who *cares*?

Charlie tried unsuccessfully to reach Kenwood by phone. Then he got in his car, drove east on Olympic, and took La Brea north toward the hills. He'd passed the Lava Lounge dozens of times—seen it plunked unceremoniously in that mini-mall—and in a detached sort of way was curious to see it from inside. Anyway, he needed a drink. It was ten o'clock, the place was packed, and some Sinatra imitator was crooning. With scientific exactitude, Charlie sat at the bar, consuming a brandy sidecar every twenty minutes. At 1:15, when there was no way he could drive, he called for a taxi.

Grace was getting ready for bed when she heard a car come down Spaulding and stop in front of the building. The night was woolly and otherwise silent, but for the drone of air conditioners. Grace heard the car door open and slam, and then the clack of footsteps coming up the path. "Please don't let it be Ian," she whispered to herself, and crept to the front window to see. Outside, a taxi pulled away from the curb, and Charlie walked drunkenly toward the building's entryway, his steps exaggerated and overly precise. A low droning sound accompanied his passage; as she listened, Grace realized he was talking to himself. My God, she thought, and without a second's hesitation she headed downstairs.

She got to the bottom of the stairwell just as Charlie began trying to fit his key into the lock. His eyes were red and bleary, and Grace could smell booze on him from ten feet away. He was still mumbling and was oblivious to her presence. "Hey," she said as quietly as she could manage. When he turned, she smiled. "Are you all right?" "Yeah," he said. "Fine." He kept trying to work the lock, but no matter what he did, the cylinder's logic eluded him.

Grace was on the verge of opening the door for him, when all of a sudden he hurled the keys to the ground. "Goddammit!" he yelled. "Fuck, fuck, fuck, fuck, fuck." Across the street a light switched on, and Grace could see a curtain drawn back to make room for a pair of eyes. From Navaro's apartment came the creak of floorboards. "Maybe we should get you inside." She tried to work her hand under Charlie's elbow but he twisted away. He seemed about to protest further, but then his shoulders deflated and his head sunk down on his neck, and it was all he could do to remain upright. "I just ..." he mumbled, his voice softer than a whisper, his body limp at Grace's touch. "Shhh," she said. "Don't worry." His keys glittered where he had thrown them, and Grace picked them up as they started up the stairs.

Grace sat Charlie on her couch and went into the kitchen, where she started brewing coffee and spread some store-bought cookies on a plate. With Ian spending less time here, the place was neater and better stocked; she'd grown used to finding things where she'd left them, of being able to enjoy what she'd bought. There were nights, of course, when her empty living room seemed as expansive and lonely as Siberia. But on this night, all that seemed part of someone else's life.

Grace set the coffee and cookies on a tray, and carried the whole arrangement into the living room. She couldn't help laughing at herself. All her life, she'd strived for distance from her mother's domesticity. Yet here she was, *entertaining*. Still, Charlie needed something, and this was all she could think to do. He was sitting in the center of the sofa, head tilted all the way back, brow furrowed like a freshly plowed field. "Coffee?" Grace asked, and Charlie lowered his head slowly.

"Sorry," he said. Then, by way of explanation: "My grandfather. Grandfather."

"What are you talking about?"

"D'y'know my grandfather was a seismologist? D'veloped the Richter Scale. Pasadena. Pasadena. Said the earth could tell us things, if we knew how to listen."

Grace didn't know how to respond. "My grandfather's a doctor," she said. "He lives in New York."

"They have fault lines in New York."

Five minutes later he was heaving into her toilet, as she stroked his back self-consciously.

Grace awoke to the chatter of birds, and stripes of sunlight fell across the living room floor. She wasn't sure where she was. Her legs felt heavy and her neck was stiff, and she had difficulty moving. Then she realized she was still on the couch, and that Charlie was snoring lightly, with his head nuzzled into her lap. Looking at him, she felt a pleasant tingle in her loins, and wiggled a little deeper into the cushions. Soon her pleasure turned to apprehension, though, and she quickly inched out from underneath him. Way to go, Grace, she thought. Way to keep complicating your life.

Out of habit, she clicked on *Good Day L.A.*, but seconds later it was interrupted by a live newscast carrying some kind of breaking story. We finally bombed Bosnia, she thought, or maybe the president got shot. Grace rubbed her eyes, and on the screen she could make out a graphic: two numerals and a decimal point, carved out of stone: "8.9." She looked more closely. Dan Rather looked rather grim. " … cannot say whether California will be declared an *a priori* emergency zone. Dr. Richter is the grandson of the man responsible for the scale with which we measure the force … "

Grace looked over at Charlie, and called his name. When he didn't stir, she looked back at the TV and stood motionless. Suddenly aware of her surroundings, she heard a sound from the street like bees buzzing, and went over to the window. There, Grace saw about a dozen reporters—some on the landing, others standing along the stairway and on the lawn. The one closest to her front window talked on a cellular phone and scribbled something onto a back-pocket pad. From the television Grace heard the name "Richter" come twice in succession and she turned to find Charlie's picture emblazoned on the screen. "Charlie!" she yelled, and he stirred. The first thing her next-door neighbor saw that morning was himself, on television. He looked up at her like a child, eyes wide and red. "What's going on?" he asked.

At 8:45 that morning, Michael Lipman called Ian's Silver Lake apartment and screamed into his ear. "*Seven calls* I've had in a half-an-hour, buddy boy. Seven *calls*. You better get fucking ready to be *rich*."

"What?"

"*Earthquake*, baby, earthquake! Got the newspaper?"

"Hold on." Ian pulled his blanket around him, opened the front door, checked to his left and his right, and stole the *Los Angeles Times* from the lady across the hall. "EARTHQUAKE COMING, SOURCES SAY" read the headline. Ian ran back to the phone. "Jesus."

"Is that fucking awesome?"

Ian experienced the nausea of happiness as he scanned the article.

"Charlie Richter ... " he mumbled.

"Is that fucking incredible? That fucking script'll be sold by the end of the *day*."

All Ian could muster was, "My *God*."

"Don't answer the phone, and I want you to get the fuck out of your house. Do you *understand* me? ... "

"But ... why?"

"Because if Jeffrey *Katzenberg* comes to your doorstep and offers you a hundred grand in *cash* and says, "Welcome to *Dreamworks*," you're gonna take his money. And you *shouldn't. That's* why."

When Grace and Charlie had recovered their senses, Grace began to plan. "Stay here till you're ready," she told him. "Stay all day if you like." Charlie seemed thoroughly upset, and phenomenally hungover. Still, he smiled his thanks to Grace, and, for an instant, he seemed to forget the tremendous pounding in his head.

Ian stood for a long time in his room, looking at the tattered Van Gogh print on his wall. His heart pounded so quickly that at first he thought it would seize. He was without a thought in his head, but never had he felt so *alive*. When his vital signs approached normal, he made coffee from yesterday's grounds and spread some peanut butter over stale bread. Sometime later he called Philadelphia, to McClintock & Marcus, attorneys, and told his father's secretary to pass along word that he wouldn't be going to law school after all.

EYES OF THE WORLD

THE EYES OF THE WORLD WERE UPON LOS ANGELES, AND no longer did it have anything to do with O. J. After the CES prediction—and after Caltech agreed "a major seismic event" seemed likely for the end of the year—Orenthal James Simpson was yesterday's news. The skittish were moving out of Southern California at a rate of twelve families a day, packing their station wagons and minivans and heading north to Portland or east to Phoenix and Tucson. AM radio was abuzz with the subject and wouldn't leave Charlie Richter alone. He'd stopped reading the papers and watching television, tired of seeing his face staring back at him.

The mayor, too, was feeling the heat. Publicly, he proclaimed Los Angeles "a safe and beautiful place to live." Privately, though, he watched the exodus with a mixture of desolation and fear. Eventually, he began making calls, looking for the kind of help only the federal government could give. And so it came to pass, on the morning of August 9, that the president's motorcade stopped traffic on Highland Avenue, creating a nightmare for anyone trying to hop into Burbank on the 101.

The president was in a peculiar mood. He had been shaken by the news that morning of Jerry Garcia's death. Because he *had* inhaled. The Grateful Dead's concert at the Avalon Ballroom in 1968 had made an impression on him he would always have to repudiate for political reasons. Riding in his limousine, he remembered that night's second set, when he had peaked during the drums and had been frightened by Mickey Hart's primal pounding of the tom-toms. But "Morning Dew" came and calmed the future president's heart. He'd abandoned his shoes and made his way toward the stage, where a freckle-faced girl with flowers in her hair danced next to him. Seized with presidential confidence, he had grabbed her by the waist and spent the following week with her.

As the president's limousine moved down Highland and he sat listening to "China Cat Sunflower," he decided to cancel his dinner with the mayor and stop by the candlelight vigil in Griffith Park.

The president had lunch at the Center for Earthquake Studies with Charlie Richter, but their seismological discussion lasted only three minutes. Preoccupied, the president asked quietly if Charlie had ever seen the Grateful Dead. Charlie perked up. "I took a leave of absence my junior year of college to follow them."

"No kidding?" The president put down his fork.

"How 'bout you?"

"About thirty shows," the president said. "I have like a hundred tapes. Most aren't soundboards. Twentieth generation or something. But I like the crackle."

"I can't believe it's over."

"When was your first show?" the president asked.

"Telluride, '78."

"Friday night or Saturday?"

"Saturday, I think."

"Saturday." The president leaned back and concentrated. "'Franklin's Tower,' 'Tennessee Jed,' 'Scarlet/Fire' … ?"

"That's the one …"

Ian Marcus was a millionaire. Just after the prediction, with every studio in town bidding on *Ear to the Ground*, pressure mounted for Grace to track Ian down. Ethan jumped down her throat the minute she arrived at the office. "It's your fucking *boy*friend's script," he'd told her. "Why haven't I seen it?"

You can't *buy* luck in this town, she thought. Like William Goldman says: "Nobody knows *anything* ..."

The deal had closed a few minutes before midnight, in a booth at Jones. What a *nightmare*. Michael Lipman, one of the world's great assholes, was having the time of his life. And, Grace knew, there's nothing worse than an ecstatic asshole. Ian didn't say a single word, just sipped champagne and performed calculations on a legal pad. Once, he leaned over and French-kissed her. How could she refuse?

Grace made one last call to business affairs, asking if they'd go as high as seven figures. She was told the president of the studio was reading the script, or skimming it anyway, and it was almost an hour before he consented to spend a million dollars to buy *Ear to the Ground* for Ethan Carson.

By midday on August 9, several FM stations were playing nothing but Grateful Dead, but the AM talk shows continued to feature earthquake commentary. At CES, the mayor and the president made a joint statement, separated by a beaming Caruthers. Then the president disappeared into the Prediction Lab, where he sat telling Charlie funny stories about the *Europe '72* tour. Soon they were nearly friends, and Charlie was invited to accompany him to Griffith Park.

As the president's motorcade cut through traffic and turned left into the park, Deadheads gawked at the sleek black limos, wondering what industry bigwigs had decided to make the scene. Around the carousel, thousands of people had gathered: gauze-draped girls whirring among bare-chested boy-men who wailed and beat bongo drums.

The president watched quietly for a few minutes, and signaled to his driver that it was time to move on. Charlie laid a hand on his arm.

"I think I'm going to stay," he said.

The president smiled and shook his hand. "Of course."

Charlie watched the motorcade pull away. He took off his jacket and loosened his tie, and hiked over the rise of grass toward the carousel. Halfway down the slope, a girl about twenty looked up. She wore a tie-dyed dress and had a long braid down her back.

"Hey," she said.

Charlie stopped.

"I know who you are. But you don't have to talk about it."

He smiled.

"You should take off your shoes," she said, then turned up the music on a tape deck next to her. From the speaker, Jerry's voice rose, strained, struggling to reach the high notes:

> *"Wake now, discover that you are the song*
> *that the morning brings.*
> *But the heart has its seasons, its evening, and*
> *thoughts of its own."*

REASONABLE DOUBT

THE GOVERNOR SAT, FEET UP, LOOKING AT HIS DESK DIARY and counting weeks until the New Hampshire primary. He hated the word "gubernatorial." It reminded him of "goober," a term his adolescent son had used to describe a moron or geek. More important, the governor was concerned with *ends*, and "gubernatorial" stank of *means*. Humming a few bars of "Hail to the Chief," he called in his speechwriter and demanded the fruits of that morning's labor.

Fresh out of Yale, the kid never shaved. But the cunning little bastard would cut his own grandmother's throat if she stood in the way of something he wanted. The governor loved that, happy to have someone so ruthless on his team.

"We go with a neg," the kid said.

"That's what I was thinking." The governor nodded.

"We crush the earthquake. We crush the president and all the liberals. We support the mayor and the citizens. And we offer prayer as an answer, but only in closing."

"Subtle."

"Soft."

"Subversive."

"God bless California. God bless America," said the governor, filling his chest with air.

"Practicing again?"

"Don't be a smartass."

At Warner Brothers Studios, on the second floor of Producer's Building Seven, at the Tailspin Pictures conference table, sat the Finnish action director Henny Rarlin, whose blockbuster movie *Die Hard as a Rock* had earned him a place on the Hollywood A-minus list. A moment ago, Ethan Carson had tried to impress him by speaking some Finnish. No go. Seated on Ethan's left was Grace, and next to her sat the newest member of the Million Dollar Spec Club. Ian wore tiny round tortoise-shell Armani eyeglasses which, he thought, made him look terribly intelligent. The three of them waited for Henny Rarlin to finish a heated conversation on his cellular phone.

"Why? Why, why, why?" he asked the apparatus. Then, loudly: "Well don't call me until you fucking *know*." He snapped his cellular before turning to the others and announcing, "I haven't read the script."

Ethan, Grace, and Ian grimaced appropriately.

"But I love earthquakes. I made some notes."

"Notes?" Ian took off his glasses. "But you haven't read the *script*."

"Ian …" Grace tried.

"I don't need to read your fucking …"

"Now, now." Ethan began to kiss some Finnish ass.

Henny Rarlin stood up and towered over Ian. "Lemme tell you something, you little *child*. You sold your script to *Varner* Brothers. They bought it for Tailspin Pictures. Now it belongs to *me*."

Ian tried to swallow.

"Ian …" Grace tried again.

"You shut up," he told her. "A week ago you wouldn't even *show* the goddamn thing."

"Not here, Ian …"

"What are they fighting about? What are you fighting about?" Henny Rarlin wanted to know.

"Nothing," Ethan said. "Creative differences."

"I am the director. Who are *they* to be having creative differences?"

The room fell silent. Ian fiddled with his glasses. With his eyes, Ethan told Grace to apologize. Right. This is business, she realized. And sometimes business *sucks*. But then she caught a glimpse of Ian, his expression so smug it nearly knocked her off her chair. You asshole, she thought, and before she could stop herself, she hissed, "If it weren't for Charlie's prediction, nobody would've *looked* at your fucking script." Then she got up and stormed out of the room.

Grace was so angry she could barely see the road. She shouldn't have walked out like that, but all she could think about was breaking up with Ian as soon as she got home. Seven months she'd given to that obnoxious come-lately, and she'd be damned if she'd give any more.

When she turned west onto Franklin, Grace was thoroughly blinded by the setting sun. She pulled to the curb, rooted around in her bag for sunglasses, looked up, and saw a 7-Eleven located conveniently before her. The next thing she remembered was paying for a pack of Merits and getting back into the car. For old time's sake, she pushed in the dashboard lighter, tore off the cellophane and aluminum wrapping, and tried to retrieve a cigarette before the contraption popped out. Grace examined the lighter's glowing tip before giving life to the Merit hanging from her lips. She smoked without shifting position and felt a dizziness that soon passed. Then she lit another and, refreshed, pulled back into traffic. And so, in a time of need, Grace had been reunited with an old friend.

"We live in an age of sound bites and media hype." The governor smiled across his audience, meeting every attending pair of eyes. "It has become possible to transmit and receive information alarmingly quickly—to compose quickly, send quickly, receive quickly, and, sadly, *react* quickly. I read everything printed about this sensational prediction, really dug there in the science. But I'm shaking my head. And I've been talking to a lot of people who're shaking their heads, too. Scientists and scholars and heads of universities—they think it's hullabaloo. But the media spun it into a story, and with that story, they sell papers. I'm all for enterprise, but what we pay for when we buy newspapers, or when we're watching the news on television, is the *truth*. So I say, if there's an earthquake coming, let it be proven beyond a reasonable doubt—in this nation, under God, with liberty. Because in the world of speculation and sensationalism, *there is no justice for all*. God bless California. And God bless the United States of America."

THEY ALL LAUGHED

EARTHQUAKES MEANT BIG MONEY. STERLING CARUTHERS knew that. Loma Prieta had paid off sixteen billion dollars, and Northridge had come through for thirty. The key, Caruthers thought, was in knowing how to make devastation work for you.

He sat in his office at the Center for Earthquake Studies pondering just that, watching stock quotations and real estate prices scroll down his computer screen. Both were declining steadily, but he knew there was a way to make a killing from it all. There must be a passage through those numbers, a pathway to exorbitant wealth. It was just a matter of solving the equations, of studying the situation until the proper combinations made themselves known.

Caruthers thought about the moguls. What would they have done? The Chandlers, the Dohenys, the Harrison Gray Otises. Men of vision, he thought, who made a killing in the San Fernando Valley, way back in 1904. Caruthers sat in his swivel chair, and praised the science that had brought him to the threshold of an opportunity this large. Watching columns of numbers cascade on his monitor, he opened his mind to the world of speculation, lighter than air.

But Charlie Richter lived in the world of doubt and deliberation, and suffered from the disease of integrity. Was predicting earthquakes any better than snooping around, telling someone her husband or his wife was unfaithful? Was he providing a *service*? Or just gossiping scientifically, on a global scale?

Whatever the case, in the past week he had come to be perceived as a doomsayer, less a scientist than a hack. First came the governor's speech, and now everyone from Maggie Murphy to Jay Leno found fault with Charlie's work. What a laugh! Suddenly, everybody was a seismologist.

More than ever before, Charlie lived and breathed and slept with his numbers. At the moment, in fact, he was eating with them—at the bar of the Authentic Café. What could he do, he wondered, to prove this earthquake beyond a reasonable doubt? And what did "reasonable doubt" mean? As a legal expression it referred to past events, but Charlie was venturing into the future. What could he do when everyone was so numerically illiterate?

Charlie left his wonderings and looked up. He didn't expect to *see* anything, but there, across the dining room, was Grace, having dinner with a long-haired man of unknown identity. Charlie wondered if she had spotted him earlier, when she'd come in; and then he considered what she'd do if their eyes were suddenly to meet. It was a game he played to test a woman's love, a silly and unscientific game, but Charlie played it anyway. And this time, he won. Grace covered her mouth with a napkin and jumped up from her chair. When she excused herself, her companion looked concerned.

Charlie stood as Grace approached somewhat defensively.

"Are you OK?" she asked him. "I tried to call you." She looked back at her table and smiled.

"It's been …" Charlie suddenly felt depressed.

"Ian and I broke up."

"Really?" He brightened, but without letting her see. Then she noticed Charlie noticing the long-haired man.

"It's business," she told him. "A film maker."

"When did you and Ian …?"

"This morning."

He smiled. "How many times have you two broken up?"

"Don't make fun of me, Charlie."

Henny Rarlin got up then and strode across the restaurant, embarrassed that a man of his stature would be left sitting alone. Grace explained to Charlie that Henny had made *Die Hard as a Rock*. He thrust his hand into Charlie's and spit out his name like an Uzi fires bullets. Then, he took Grace by the elbow and tried to steer her toward their table.

"What are you doing?" she said, and pulled away.

Diners looked up as Henny Rarlin ranted. "Are you having dinner with him, or *me*!?" Charlie gestured for his check, and Rarlin said something he couldn't hear. Grace slapped the film maker's face, and stalked out of the restaurant. It all happened so quickly, Charlie just laughed.

It was laughter, probably, that gave him the idea. His body's convulsing, the release of tension, the movement of unnoticed muscles. Five minutes later, at a pay phone on Beverly, Charlie called someone at ABC News. Then he jumped into his car and headed east on the 10.

Outside of Indio, he saw them—the vans, the crews. A helicopter hovered. When he pulled up, a sea of microphones came through his driver-side window, so he told the one about the Pirate and the Parrot, and they all laughed.

Looking closely at his watch, Charlie got out of his car, stood on a mound of dirt, and put his arms in the air till the crowd quieted down. "It's gonna be between a 3.1 and a 3.3," he announced. "Right where you're standing." A cacophony resulted, and twenty reporters hurled questions at Charlie. "One at a time!" he shouted. He turned to a sober-looking blonde whose hair appeared frozen to her head. "Yes?" he smiled.

But before she could say a word, the rumbling began.

BEDTIME STORIES

EMMA GRANT SAT ON THE EDGE OF HER NINE-YEAR-OLD daughter Dorothy's bed, tucking the child in. It was 9:30, and Dorothy was yawning, but Emma lingered, taking her time. She had lived all her life in this house in Northridge, but lately she had begun to worry about the windows with their cheap little slats of glass, and the building's shoddy wooden frame. Now, staring at her daughter, she had a momentary flash of panic and, for the millionth time, felt a phantom rumbling in the ground.

The house was a one-family ranch, shielded from the street by a ragged spray of bougainvillea, with a postage stamp yard that was unkempt and long. When Emma's parents bought it, thirty years ago, Northridge had been on the outer rim of Los Angeles's suburbs, its wide, clean streets full of kids on bicycles and dads mowing the lawn after work. These days, the whole place looked like a construction site, with stacks of lumber and mountains of gravel piled up in driveway after driveway, the sounds of drills and hammers punctuating the air like the calls of angry birds. Only a few blocks away, condemned apartment complexes had been taken over by squatters and gangs, and the boulevards were littered with broken glass. It had gotten so Emma wouldn't let Dorothy outside alone anymore. But whenever she pestered Henry to pull up stakes, he reminded her they'd just spent a fortune rebuilding.

Emma's family had meant for it to be their starter house, but they had never moved on. Her parents had paid off the mortgage, and then died. And Emma couldn't help feeling she had taken over their lives.

Her reverie was interrupted by what sounded like the chirping of a bird. Good, she thought, birds never chirp if there's a shaker coming, but then the noise came again. It was Dorothy, sitting up in bed, eyes rheumy with exhaustion.

"Mom?"

Emma shook away her thoughts. "What?"

"Could you please let me go to sleep?"

In the living room, the Dodger game flickered across the TV. Nomo on the mound; Henry on the sofa. His big feet hung over the armrest like hams—but Emma could tell by the regular sound of his breathing that he was asleep. Sure enough, when she stepped through the doorway from the hall and came around the side, his eyes were closed, and his stomach rose and fell evenly, like a piston engine. She raised her eyes to the incomplete molding at the top of the walls. He'd been promising to finish it since January but, every night, after he drained four or five MGD Lights, he'd pass out on the couch. Molding forgotten, another promise left unkept.

"Henry." Emma kicked the sofa, and he stirred with a groan.

"Huh?" He rubbed his eyes. "Time is it?"

"Almost ten."

"Rough day."

It was always a rough day for Henry, a rough week, a rough year, a rough life. Today he'd poured concrete on a job site, and hopefully tomorrow he'd be back out there again. Still …

"You gonna finish that molding, Henry?"

"I said it was a rough day."

"The washer's still broken; you said you'd fix that, too …"

"Come on, Em. Gimme a break in my own damn house."

"Jesus."

"What?"

"Nothing."

"Say it."

She took a deep breath and ran her hands down the front of her dress. "We'll never sell if the work's not done."

"We're not selling."

"If that earthquake comes ..."

"Let it come." He stood up and headed down the hall.

Emma walked around the house turning off lights. She got a beer and sat down on the couch. She flipped channels for a few minutes, before landing on the news. The top five stories were about the coming earthquake.

She sat rigid, eyes fixed on the screen. Her stomach tensed during an interview with a man who was moving his family east. In the background a minivan waited, full of children and clothes. Watching him, Emma's heart started racing, and she began to feel the way she might if she were contemplating her own death—nauseated, overwhelmed, as if everything she had, or was, was only a dream.

She clicked off the television and paced, checking the bolts that held everything to the walls. She pushed against the TV, making sure it, too, was fixed in place.

In her dreams, the television was always the first thing to go. Usually, Dorothy was still a baby, crawling around in front of it, laying her little hands across the screen. As it came crashing down, Emma could do nothing but watch. She would wake up in a cold sweat, gasping for equilibrium, as if the world had flipped inside out.

In Dorothy's room, Emma watched her daughter's gentle breathing. Then she headed to the kitchen for another beer. On the table was a stack of bills.

Oh God, she thought, and sat to keep from falling. It was going to be a long night.

THURSDAY NIGHT, PART TWO

SOME FRIDAY MORNING, TAKE SANTA MONICA BOULEVARD to work and get a load of the cars in the Formosa's parking lot. They don't serve breakfast there, but you can bet they served a whole lot of booze the night before. The place is packed Thursday nights with twentysomethings who haven't learned how to drink. Or maybe they've learned how to drink but not how to hold their drink. Maybe they have something to drink about, some sad thing, some loss. They can't find work. They work too hard. Or they work and work but don't make a dime. Then again, maybe they're worried about the earthquake.

As the waitress approached, Grace thwapped back the spittle of her Amstel Light and ordered another round. *She wasn't worried about the earthquake, or anything else, because she knocked on Charlie's door every other night,* for the latest science, the latest anything, whatever. She wanted to be near him. Kiss him. But she couldn't bring herself to make the first move. What if he'd never even considered it? It would kill her if Charlie got this shocked look on his face and suddenly stopped trusting her. She had chosen, as the object of her desire, the busiest and most preoccupied man in Southern California. Still, she imagined that, when the earthquake came, she could be in his arms. What a sap I am, Grace thought. What a romantic sap.

As far as she was concerned, Ian Marcus, former sponge, present swaggerer and future prick—who was, at the moment, sitting across the room from her—didn't exist. He, on the other hand, glanced in Grace's direction often, surreptitiously as a millionaire can, or a six-fifty-against-a-million-millionaire, anyway.

He was different now. He looked better. He smiled more, and when he did, he smiled more truly, because suddenly he didn't need anything from anyone. He kissed the ass of nobody. And that can be a pretty important thing.

Ian sat talking to a guy he had once written a spec script with: a buddy comedy, set in a beach town, called *The Cape of Great Hope*. Ian had never thought much of his writing.

"Remember," the guy asked Ian, "when we talked last Christmas?"

"Last Christmas?"

"Like around Christmas? I think it was Damiano's."

"*When?*"

"We had pizza, late," the guy said. His name was Jon. Ian didn't know what he was talking about. "And you got a stomachache. *Yes*, you got a stomachache."

"I think I remember."

"Do you remember what we talked about? That night you got a stomachache?"

"What?"

"We talked about *Ear to the Ground*."

Ian took a nonchalant sip of beer. "So?"

"Do you remember spe*ci*fically what we talked about in regard to *Ear to the Ground*?"

"What are you talking about, Jon?"

"Act two was basically *constructed* that night at Damiano's."

"What are you saying?"

"You *know* what I'm saying. You had them meeting on like page *eighty*, and I told you if you moved that up …"

"That's pretty simple stuff."

"What about the *scene*, Ian? I gave you the whole fucking scene with the seismologist's wife!"

Jon disgustedly got up, nodded to a few people on his way to the bar, and ordered a Maker's Mark neat. He turned once toward Ian and shook his head. Then he leaned over to an attractive woman in an old-fashioned dress.

"Do you know that the guy sitting over there is like one of my closest friends? That he just sold a script for a million dollars? And that he took an idea, took part of an idea, took *all* of an idea for an important part of his script, that just sold for a million dollars, and he won't even admit we dis*cussed* it? I say this to you not wanting any *money* from him. Even if he were to offer it to me. If he said, like, 'Here's a hundred thousand …'"

"… you wouldn't take it." The woman smiled a little.

"No, I wouldn't."

She smiled again. "Here it is, a hundred thousand." She pantomimed holding a suitcase.

"Maybe I'd take fifty." He gave her his hand. "My name's Jon, by the way."

Grace tooks the stairs to her apartment slowly. She wasn't drunk but she had eaten too little. She was exhausted and, frankly, sad. It felt like the weekend on Thursday nights at the Formosa, but Grace knew she still had to get through Friday. Suddenly she felt old, as though the once-promising flame that was her life had dimmed. Just then, Charlie opened his door, and their eyes met through his screen.

"Hey," she said, and blushed.

He pushed open the screen door. "You okay?"

She didn't answer.

"You want to come in?"

"No," she said, "let's play this scene right out here on the balcony." The minute the words came tumbling out of her mouth she couldn't believe she'd spoken them.

His eyebrows rose. He came outside, and the screen door slammed behind him. "Is this a *balcony*?" he asked. And before she lost her nerve, she leaned in and kissed him. Then, without a word, she turned away, went inside her apartment, and went to bed.

THE CHILDREN'S HOUR

DOROTHY REMEMBERED BEING LOST SOMEWHERE BEFORE the gauzy filaments of sleep were rended by what felt like an explosion. She remembered a loud bang, and then what sounded like the thudding of horse hooves, coming closer. She remembered looking for the horses, but seeing only black; there had been a crash like thunder, and she remembered opening her eyes.

Dorothy remembered spinning, as if a tornado had picked up her entire house and cast it carelessly to the ground. She remembered how the walls seemed crooked against the black, star-swept sky. She'd wondered how the stars could be so close; how they had crept through the ceiling into her room. She remembered the pain in her arm, and not being able to move. The last thing she remembered was her mother's face, hanging over her own—a face wild as the moon, her mouth a red gash, crying, "Oh God, my little girl!"

It all seemed like a dream twenty months later, except for a small scar above Dorothy's right elbow and aches that came and went with the rain. Then, this afternoon, while she played a game called Prom, with her Barbies on the living room floor, she remembered it again. Henry had been stretched out on the couch in his pajamas, face flush with flu, when they interrupted *Ricki Lake* to announce a 5.5 near Barstow, somewhere called China Lake. Dorothy's mother had been laughing, but as she watched the news flash, her face drained of color.

"See?" she hissed at Henry.

He turned onto his side. "For God's sake, Emma. We didn't even feel it."

"*This* time."

Dorothy took the dolls into her room. Then she came back and stood by the door. "I'm going out."

Her mother's eyes flickered across the television screen, where a seismograph traced aftershocks in waves. "Where?"

"The park. I wanna climb a tree."

"Be careful. And you *stay* in the park."

Dorothy wheeled her bike into the driveway where, through the living room window, she could hear an argument revving up. She pedaled onto the sidewalk toward the park, past two abandoned buildings and another one under reconstruction.

They had spent two weeks in the park after the earthquake, living in a four-person Army tent, jumping up each time an aftershock shook the aluminum struts like so much Christmas tinsel. They ate canned food and shat in outhouses. There'd been hundreds of families, and kids running around, screaming in the mud, but Dorothy had been in a fresh cast and had missed most of the fun.

This afternoon, the park was barricaded. Dorothy watched as work crews swarmed the field; bulldozers and cranes had chewed the grass into a fine green pulp. Workmen operated a steamshovel next to a huge old sycamore, digging a trench at the root line.

A man in a hardhat and blue FEMA windbreaker materialized and spoke to Dorothy in a soft Southern twang. "Stay behind the line, honey."

"What are you doing with that tree?"

"Bringing it down."

"Why?"

"Clearin' the field."

"Why?"

"Instructions."

"You're afraid of the earthquake. Like maybe the trees'll fall down."

"Look, little girl …"

"My whole life I played in this park."

"Well, you can't play here now."

Henry and Emma were still arguing when Dorothy got home, so she leaned her bike against the summer-singed bougainvillea and went around to the backyard. Her fort stood in the center of the grass.

The fort was little more than a lean-to, built of discarded materials Henry had scavenged for her from various construction sites. Inside, there was a stool and a wooden box for a table. She pretended some rusty aluminum casing was a stove, and near it an upturned milk crate served as a cradle for her favorite doll, a red-headed baby named Samantha. Dorothy sat down and rocked the cradle, leaning in and brushing the doll's hair back with her hand. Gently, she pulled a thin strip of green cloth up under her chin.

"Still sleeping, Samantha? Don't you wanna hear a story?" The doll looked up with blank glass eyes.

"Once upon a time there was a nine-year-old girl named Dorothy, who lived in Northridge, California. She had the power to move the earth."

Dorothy got up slowly and moved to the exact center of the room. Placing her hands at the corners of the fort's patchy roof, she began to shake the structure for all it was worth.

"Earthquake! Earthquake!" she shouted. "Oh baby, cover your head!"

Dorothy flung the cradle across the room, doing a spastic dance as she pretended to keep herself from falling. Samantha ended up crumpled in a corner, arms and legs splayed.

Dorothy lunged over to where the doll lay. She picked it up and held it in her arms, pressing the plastic flesh to her own. Tears welled in her eyes.

"Oh God," she cried. "My little girl!"

AND JUSTICE FOR ALL

CHARLIE WAS IN THE PREDICTION LAB, STARING INTO THE ash-gray glow of his computer screen, when word began to circulate throughout the Center for Earthquake Studies that a verdict had come down in the Simpson case. The whole beehive was abuzz: Secretaries chattered to each other animatedly, and technicians gathered in front of a small color TV, flipping back and forth between the Angels' sudden-death playoff against the Mariners and CNN. Eventually, someone in the office started collecting money for a gambling pool, noting people's predictions carefully in a ledger. The wagering had nothing to do with baseball; innocent or guilty—that was the question.

Charlie liked to think of himself as the one person in Los Angeles who couldn't have cared less. He had not watched the trial on television, nor read the stories about Marcia Clark's hairdo. He didn't give a damn about Lance Ito's hourglasses, and he wouldn't have recognized Mark Fuhrman if the detective had waved a blood-stained glove in his face.

He'd met Simpson as a kid, when Charlie's grandfather had taken him to see the Heisman Trophy winner play at USC. After the game, they'd been escorted into the locker room, and O. J. had signed young Charlie's program: "O. J. Simpson, number 32." There had been something flat and distant in O. J.'s eyes—shark's eyes, rolling over from gray to black. Charlie had gone home and put that program in the back of his closet. Years later, he finally threw it away.

Now, from what little Charlie knew or cared, O. J. Simpson had killed his ex-wife and also the man who'd seen him do it. He had left his own blood at the crime scene and had carried the blood of his victims back to his home. What could be more scientific or empirical than that?

Still, Charlie felt a twinge of curiosity, as if his indifference had somehow unraveled and worked its way inside him like a tangle of worms. He tried to focus on the screen, but soon he pushed away from his work station and went over to where the technicians still clustered and conjectured around the TV.

"Hey, Charlie. You want a piece of this?"

Charlie pulled out a bill. "Guilty," he said. "On both counts."

Tuesday morning, for the first time in a long time, there were no reporters waiting on the sidewalk in front of Charlie's apartment. Navaro sat in the early mist smoking a Pall Mall on the steps, and he gave a small laugh as Charlie came outside.

"Look at you," said the landlord, sweeping his arm across the empty lawn. "Yesterday's news."

"Yeah," Charlie said, stopping at the bottom of the stoop. "Too bad they won't stay away."

Navaro took a long drag off his cigarette and exhaled a ghostlike spray of smoke into the air. "He's gonna walk. You know that?"

"I don't think so."

"Ever heard of 'reasonable doubt'?"

Was there nothing else to talk about? Charlie wondered. Nothing at all?

"Four *hours*," Navaro continued. "You don't condemn a man in four hours."

"Maybe you're right." Charlie started walking.

"Eight million of my tax dollars, pissed away ..."

"Yeah, well ..."

"Justice!" Navaro spat on the pavement. "No such thing as justice with these lawyers running *wild*. That Johnnie Cochran's got everybody so worried about a riot they forget two people got their throats cut!" The angry old man's voice got low. "All you need is money in this world. Y'got money, you can kill whoever you want."

At nine-fifty on the morning of October 3, the city of Los Angeles drew a sharp collective breath of anticipation, then grew silent as a tomb. Television sets emerged from office desk drawers, and workers gathered before them with the reverence of the faithful. In bedrooms and living rooms and kitchens they watched, as the honorable Judge Ito welcomed the jury into the courtroom for the last time, and O. J.'s granite jaw quivered and was still. They watched while they drove the freeways, or sat down in restaurants, and on the sidewalks; they saw the images multiplied in the windows of appliance stores. They watched and they waited, until the bailiff stumbled: "In the matter of the people versus Oren ... Orenthal James Simpson ..."

Afterward, Charlie looked around at his colleagues. He saw the elation of some and the dismay of others. To his surprise, he found that he felt sick—and not because he'd lost five dollars. No, in the absence of another suspect, it was as if the killings had never taken place.

Later, Charlie would consider the verdict to have caused its own kind of earthquake, ripping through the soul of the city with a palpable seismic force. And for a few days afterward, as jurors made appearances on daytime talk shows, it became clear that this trial had shaken a divided nation. How ironic, Charlie thought, that in eighty-seven days, quite something else would shake and divide the ground beneath their feet.

GREEN MEANS GO

GRACE GONGLEWSKI SPENT EARLY OCTOBER IN THE conference room at Tailspin Pictures, playing host to producers and associate producers and assistant producers and line producers and co-executive producers, production managers and post-production supervisors, explosives experts and special effects designers, directors of photography and camera assistants and assistant camera assistants, location scouts, location coordinators, and George Lucas.

Top brass at Warner Brothers popped in twice a day to say hello and give their full support to the most ambitious project in the studio's history: A feature film from script to theaters in seventy days. Less than three weeks into pre-production, not including core salaries, two million dollars had been spent on *Ear to the Ground*, primarily, it seemed, on doughnuts, coffee, and Wolfgang Puck gourmet pizzas.

Five separate first-units would film simultaneously, and a helicopter would shuttle the director and actors among them. Six hundred crew members and six thousand extras would be employed. A tidal wave would be enacted, freeways collapsed, and—at last count—eight high-rises would be swallowed whole. Three thousand walkie-talkies were to be rented, along with three hundred on-road and off-road vehicles. And three *million* feet of film would be exposed. Editing would begin the minute film was shot. Six months of work would be collapsed into one, at a cost of a hundred million dollars. And rising.

When Grace's alarm went off at six-fifteen on Friday morning, her eyes and lids had fused, and it took a combination of Visine, saline, and water to separate them. Once upon a time, she had looked forward to Fridays, but the bleary-eyed reality was that she wouldn't have a day off until the new year.

Casting began today, and Grace hated nothing more than seeing three hundred people deliver the same stupid lines differently, over and over. She hated casting directors, especially the parties they threw, where empty-headed beauties were just waiting to get your card so they could call you at the office. Actors were nightmares, not to be trusted. Their *talent* was to be whoever you wanted them to be. In that regard, she thought, they were nothing.

There were a hundred pretty actresses gathered outside a soundstage near the Burton Way gate. The cavernous interior had been divided by screens, which didn't make the place seem any more intimate. Grace was well into her fourth cup of coffee when Ian walked onto the stage.

"Have you seen Henny this morning?" he asked Grace.

She shook her head.

"Have you talked to him?"

"No."

Ian's cell phone rang.

"Hello?" he said.

Grace tried not to watch him, but she couldn't help herself. Ian seemed so fulfilled, like a butterfly that had emerged from a cocoon. She tried to remember how he used to be—pale, unkempt, eyes always looking for an angle to play. Now, he seemed possessed of a preternatural calm that radiated from his face and shoulders in exponentially increasing waves. He wasn't even rattled when Henny Rarlin stalked onto the stage and told him to get off the phone.

"The pages *suck*," Henny bellowed. "You haven't incorporated one …"

Ian pulled half a dozen sheets of script from an expensive black-leather shoulder bag and handed them to the director. "You must've read the *old* ones," he announced.

Henny grabbed the pages, pulled a pair of John Lennon glasses from his pocket, and wound them dramatically over his ears. Then he began to read.

When word got around that Henny Rarlin had arrived, at least ten actresses found a reason to draw near. But Henny, ever the leerer, interrupted his reading for only a second before he returned to the script. Turning a page, he smiled; he chuckled. In a gesture symbolizing his deepest concentration, he flung his arm over his head and grasped his opposite ear. A moment later, he smiled broadly to Ian.

"This sucks much less," Henny said.

At Warner's, marketing usually met on Mondays, but this Friday, they were having a special session to figure out how they would ever be able to cover costs on *Ear to the Ground*. What had been publicized, even paraded, as a hundred-million-dollar movie was now *their* problem. Or, depending on how you looked at it, their challenge.

First, they condemned the costliness of special effects in general; then they discussed whether anybody really believed the Big One was coming. Most of them did. "Nobody's leaving, I hope," somebody said, in an attempt at a joke.

This much they knew: The film had to open at least two weeks before December 29. If it was a stinker, and the quake came, they'd probably be rescued. If it was a hit, and the quake came, it'd be a fucking *bonanza*.

But what if the quake didn't come? What if it was early, or late? What would happen to the *hype*? What they needed was a way to link the actual facts about the earthquake with the marketing campaign for *Ear to the Ground*. That was when

Meyer Stern, worldwide president of marketing, had the idea of calling Sterling Caruthers.

THE LOGIC OF NUMBERS

STERLING CARUTHERS HUNG UP THE PHONE AND SAT for a long time without moving any part of his body. This temporary paralysis, caused by a jolting stimulus to his pineal gland, was actually the result of a five-minute conversation that had netted him seven million dollars. Having not yet let go of the cradled receiver, and sitting still as a fly the instant before you take a swat at it, Caruthers realized that his schemes to capitalize on the coming earthquake had been merely the uncreative ideas of a desperate man. He had pushed when he should have relaxed. The Simpson trial had temporarily stolen his limelight. Now, he knew, the opportunities would come.

Caruthers suddenly remembered a "SALE" sign by that chateau on Mulholland; then he recalled a BMW commercial he'd seen on television that morning. Victoria M., the agent he'd met weeks ago at William Morris, was hopeful he could become the premier earthquake spokesman—that is, should the disaster strike. Already, there was money swirling around this quake, and the young agent had been particularly shocked to find how badly she wanted it. Nothing comparable had happened to her since coming to Hollywood, and Caruthers had been impressed at the way she'd adapted herself to the idea of cashing in on future pain and suffering. In the closing chapter of the second millennium, he thought, the smart money was squarely on doom.

The call from Warner Brothers had come out of the blue, but by the end of the week there would be dozens of calls. Perhaps hundreds. Turning down million-dollar offers suddenly seemed the most delightful of pursuits.

His brother had made scads of money in telecommunications, and his sister's husband's real-estate portfolio grew larger every Christmas. But this year, Sterling Caruthers would surpass them both. He'd stuff their stockings with hate, and with expensive little nuggets from Caldwell or Tiffany's. It'd be the worst Christmas of their lives.

Caruthers began to play a game people sometimes play when they're immobilized by their own thoughts: pretending for a moment the paralysis is real and that they'll never move again.

Then the phone rang, and Caruthers picked it up. "Victoria M. from William Morris," his secretary told him. Probably wants a commission from the Warner thing, he thought. Tough luck, sweetie.

Caruthers wondered if what he was doing was legal, making a deal to sell information to a movie studio twenty-four hours before it went to the media. Then again, if William Morris didn't seem bothered by it, how bad could it be? He let Victoria M. dangle on hold for several minutes, then proceeded to beat her up over the commission. The little bitch wouldn't yield. "At the William Morris Agency," she told him, "we're not in the practice of representing half-clients." By the time they hung up, he'd made a verbal agreement for across-the-board representation. Then Caruthers called Charlie Richter to see if there was any information on which he could trade.

Charlie sat across from Ian in the dining room of Chaya Brasserie, eating a bowl of spicy shrimp soup. Ian had called him, hoping to pick his brain on a point of science. *Ear to the Ground*, whose script was now on its ninth draft, was scheduled to go before the cameras in two weeks, at a Current

Estimated Cost (CEC) of $135 million. Industrywide chants of "Quake Gate" increased in volume and fervor whenever the studio announced a budget increase. Sour grapes, Ian knew. But now Ian knew a lot of things. He knew enough about fault lines and plate tectonics and soil samples, but he still did *not* know the simple scientific principle by which earthquakes could be predicted.

"That can't really be easily explained," Charlie told him.

"Try me."

Charlie felt a twinge of discomfort ripple through him, and he put his soup spoon down. In a certain way, he felt guilty for having been the catalyst in Grace and Ian's breakup. It was funny how things worked, he thought: A rift in a relationship could go undetected for months, just something between two people that they both ignored, like a dormant seismic fault. Then, all of a sudden, it was like there was too much alkaline in the soil.

Charlie wasn't proud of it, but he knew Grace had placed Ian and him side-by-side like suspects in a police lineup. She had released Ian on his own recognizance but had held Charlie for further questioning.

Perhaps *that* was why he'd agreed to come to lunch, to talk about Grace. But soon he felt guilty and realized how inappropriate that would be. Besides, the earth was moving underneath them *right now*; it would move differently in sixty-three days. Nauseated, he pushed his bowl away. Then he took out a mechanical pencil and proceeded to give Ian his first lesson in the logic of numbers.

PARALLEL LIVES

WHEN GRACE GONGLEWSKI GOT HOME FROM WORK ON Thursday, it was already Friday morning: two-twenty-three, according to her Honda's dashboard digital clock, its little colon blinking on and off like a pair of knowing eyes. Upstairs, her answering machine also flickered, but Grace ignored it. What she wanted most was to take off her cowboy boots and fall into a deep sleep.

Not that such a thing was likely. Not at all. Grace realized this when she went into the bedroom and fiddled with the alarm. She would be back at work in five hours. She hated her life just then, and kicked her right boot into the corner, where it ricocheted like a stray bullet before coming to rest, right side up, at the foot of her bed. Her left boot, however, went straight in the air and landed on her dresser, scattering coins and keys and assorted odds and ends.

The perfect cap to the perfect day, she thought. One endless stream of disappointments, from the moment Ethan told her she wouldn't be picking up Bridge Bridges from the airport.

"Why?" Grace said.

"I need you to collate scripts."

"How many scripts?" Grace's heart clenched.

"Five hundred. With three stages of rewrites."

"Come on, Ethan, that's an assistant's job."

"Oh?" Ethan countered. "So it's an *ego* thing."

Ever since Bridge Bridges had been cast in *Ear to the Ground*, she'd looked forward to meeting him. He was a star, a real movie star, and she loved the way, in films like *The First TV Show* and *Hairless*, his sleepy grin and piercing blue eyes lit up the screen. Grace's anticipation had increased considerably when a friend at New Line confided that Bridge was as nice as he looked. It was for moments like these, Grace thought, that she'd gotten into the movies.

But no, Grace would be collating scripts instead. And not just *any* script; *Ian's* script, the script he had written in this very living room while she was at Tailspin Pictures all day. I'm surrounded by assholes, she thought. The air around her thinned, and she almost couldn't breathe. She had a vision of a porch swing, a place where the wind rippled the leaves of trees. But the vision had no face. She was *watching* the scene from here, from this apartment, from this job, from this life. She answered to Ethan, always answered to Ethan, instead of telling him to take his sorry job and shove it up his ass.

That was the last thought Grace had before she went to sleep, and the first thing she thought about when the alarm went off at six-thirty. At seven-oh-five, the phone rang. She decided to let the machine pick it up.

"Hey, Grace," came Ian's voice. "Sorry so early, but my e-mail's down, and these pages need to go in. I'm faxing them over. Could you please input them for me?"

Grace stared gape-mouthed as the phone rang again. A moment later, a monumental length of fax paper spewed onto her floor.

Charlie got up and made coffee, then sat down at his computer and accessed the CES network. Reporters had been around the office like a swarm of bees, so he had begun to spend a lot of time at home. As he'd explained to Caruthers, it didn't matter where he did his work. And, besides, he had a new idea that, until it was better formed, he wanted to keep out of the public eye.

Charlie had begun to think about epicenters. After China Lake, he studied points of impact, tracing the ways they appeared up and down a fault. He knew there was a pattern to epicenters, and that the location of each temblor would affect other local temblors.

Charlie had tried to explain this to Caruthers at their weekly meeting. "I have an idea about epicenters that might enable us to head this thing off," he'd said.

"Head it off?" Caruthers looked confused. "You mean so the earthquake wouldn't happen?"

"It would still happen, but we might be able to deflect the shock, and the city could be spared."

Caruthers knitted his brow and folded his hands in front of his face. "How?"

Charlie explained his notion of a *retro*shock, a kind of counter-quake, explosively induced, that could neutralize the Big One.

"You want to create an explosion of nine-point magnitude?"

"Maybe."

"Are you crazy? Stop wasting your time."

Charlie knew it wasn't a waste of time. It was just that bureaucrats like Caruthers never had an ounce of vision. But with only fifty-six days left …

His thoughts were interrupted by the chiming of his doorbell. Who would bother him so early in the day? When he opened the door, he discovered Grace, her eyes sparkling like two diamonds in a pool. She carried orange juice, champagne, and a bag of pastries.

"On your way to work?" Charlie asked.

"I was," she said, walking inside as the screen slammed shut behind her. "But then I quit my fucking job."

COLLABORATION THERAPY

MOVIES ARE LIKE RAILROAD TRAINS: HEAVY, BULKY, AND difficult to get started. Their locomotives are powered by hundred-dollar bills shoveled into furnaces by worsted-wool workadays at business affairs. A switchmaster sits at every junction, a production executive waiting to pull a lever, to affect the train's course.

Like the worst cinematic catastrophes, train wrecks are the result of missed communication. Switchmaster error can cause two trains to collide, or send one of them over a cliff. Sometimes the only way to avoid this is to apply the emergency brakes, scraping steel against steel, rods against cylinders, sending sparks into the air. Hence the expression "grinding to a halt."

Grace Gonglewski quit her job at seven-fifteen on Friday morning, and by seven-thirty, *Ear to the Ground* had begun to shut down. The process started with Ian, whose pages could not be input, and thus were not turned in. It moved from him to Henny who, without the pages, could not run his actors through the new scenes. Ethan heard about the problem early but, unable to reach Grace, could do nothing about it. Instead, he spent much of the day reassuring Bob Semel, chairman of Warner Brothers, that everything was fine.

There were other difficulties as well: When it came to the train called *Ear to the Ground*, Grace, more than anyone, had been the driver. Among the engineers, she alone understood the machine. She knew the chain of command because she had created it. And by leaving, she threatened to destroy it.

Ehrich Weiss came from Mannheim to Hollywood in 1977, freshly Ph.D'd in psychology. He was handsome and blond, and possessed a raucous but genuine laugh. Soon, wealthy humorists were diving onto his couch, trying out new material as they investigated their pasts. In front of Ehrich they fell hilariously to pieces, so they invited him to their parties. They gave him small roles in their films. He dated actresses. By 1981, Weiss was known as a hack.

Then he fell ill with cancer, a rare form that targeted his blood without localizing its attack. His chances were slim, the doctors said. "It would be wise," they advised, "if you'd let us experiment." So he submitted to a painful process called hydrative therapy. His blood was thickened and thinned, its volume reduced and increased. Chemicals were injected. Readings taken, smears smeared.

From his hospital bed, Ehrich wrote a book entitled *Relationships: A Collaboration*. And after a month his condition improved. A simple diet and serious work restored him. He went home with his strength and, perhaps more miraculously, his dignity.

He married Hillary Semel, sister of Bob Semel. Soon he became a close friend of the entire Warner Brothers family, and when Martin Long had his legendary tiff with director Jon Lansid, Ehrich was brought in to smooth things over. The men were hugging in less than an hour. Ehrich became Warner's vice president for psychology in 1991.

Four years later, Grace Gonglewski, Ethan Carson, Ian Marcus, and Henny Rarlin were in Dr. Weiss's office on the Warner lot, waiting to begin Collaboration Therapy. There was little conversation among them. Instead, there was that element of negotiation where no party wished to spill before another did. It had taken some doing to get them together, and no one wanted to be the first to play his hand. With *Ear to the Ground* scheduled to begin shooting in twenty-four hours, confusion abounded.

Ethan sat in the first chair by the door, checking his watch every few seconds. He could hardly bring himself to look at Grace. He would have fired her if she hadn't already quit, and he would never have asked her back if Bob Semel hadn't demanded her presence on the set. She was a D-girl, for Christ's sake, and now he had to kowtow to her? We'll see about that, Ethan thought, and examined his watch again.

Next to him, Ian wondered whether he'd have time to keep his rendezvous with the blonde from the Craft Services truck. There were advantages to being the writer of a blockbuster script, but he'd been working too hard to enjoy them. Now he had to deal with *this*. He looked over at Henny, but the director just seemed bored.

Grace stood alone by the windows, her back to the others. All week, she had ignored messages from Ethan, even as they grew increasingly desperate. What concern was it of hers if *Ear to the Ground* became a multimillion-dollar flop? In a certain sense, Grace believed in karma, and if you thought that way, Ethan was getting his. Stuck in the middle of production, watching it fall to pieces, with his starched shirt collar finally slicing through the tender skin of his neck.

But then Bob Semel had called her and explained how much he wanted her around. If she would return, he would consider it a personal favor, and personal favors were always repaid. Exactly what that meant had yet to be determined, but Grace knew she had been noticed, and that she was finally in position to leave *these* three assholes behind.

Grace was interrupted by a door swishing open on well-oiled hinges, and the padding of Ehrich Weiss's expensive loafers across the floor. The doctor nodded at no one in particular, then took a seat behind his desk. "Act one," he announced, "getting to know you." When no one uttered so much as a hello, he spread his hands and said, "Let's not all talk at once."

A MODEL WORLD

LOUIS NAVARO ROSE AT SEVEN-FIFTEEN THURSDAY morning to the sound of a Skilsaw buzzing through wood. At first, he just pulled the pillow over his head and tried to go back to sleep, but then he realized the noise was coming from his own backyard. He raised his body out of bed slowly and grabbed a ribbed undershirt and a pair of workpants. Then, lighting a Pall Mall and coughing the day's first cough, he headed outside to see what the hell was going on.

In the yard, he discovered Charlie Richter, covered in sawdust and dirt, fitting a long two-by-four into what looked like an oversized frame. It was an oddly shaped construction, and Navaro noticed another, parallel structure already put together and leaning up against the house.

Navaro cleared his throat. "Little early in the day for this, wouldn't you say?"

Charlie jumped at the sound of his landlord's voice. "Oh, Mr. Navaro. Sorry if I disturbed you."

"Disturbed me?" Navaro took another pull off his cigarette and threw it to the ground. "You woke me *up*. What the ..."

"It's a model," Charlie said.

"A model. Just what I was thinking."

"It's the San Andreas, see? A replica. I'm going to rig a generator ..."

"Yeah, yeah," Navaro said, lighting his second cigarette.

"You do that. But do me a favor, will ya?"

Charlie nodded.

"Don't be sawing any wood before nine."

Exactly six days later, Charlie finished his model, and stood over it like a god. Before him lay a panorama of the desert that was so realistic it could have been used as a miniature set for *Ear to the Ground*. The two wooden forms had been fitted into the frame, filled with dirt and earth, and landscaped to replicate the barren crags and rocky hillocks outside San Bernardino. Charlie had even included lichen and small bushes to approximate desert growth.

The entire structure stood on a platform supported by sawhorses, beneath which sat a small gasoline generator and a system of pulleys and winches. When Charlie tested the machinery, the effect was quite convincing: As pressure built, the forms began to grind until, with a rip, they slid apart, rending the earth of this model world. It was exactly what would happen on December 29th. Exactly what was happening *already* under the ground.

Then Charlie went about setting up the charge. By his side were plastic explosives, which he lifted gingerly from a corrugated box. When the time came, he would have to know the exact direction of the slippage, which would determine the direction of the neutralizing charge. This was the wild card and, in the end, he'd have to make an educated guess. For now, the only question was simply whether or not a retroshock would work.

Charlie took the packs of explosives and joined them to create a single, or *united,* charge. Out of one end ran an electronic fuse, controlled by remote; out of the other was a *detonator pin* which would conduct and focus the explosive charge, with pinpoint accuracy, to a specific place in the model's crevice.

When the wiring was complete, Charlie carried the remote to a far corner of the yard. It was only then that he realized he had forgotten, for quite some time, to breathe. He looked up and noticed the way the sky crested above the treetops and extended upward, out of reach. It felt like the moment before a thunderstorm, the moment before a fight. "OK," Charlie whispered, as if a normal tone of voice would detonate the charge.

Then he flipped the switch, and all hell broke loose.

The call came in at three-seventeen—an explosion at 418 North Spaulding Avenue. Parked in the lot at Canter's, having a cup of coffee and eating a knish, Officer Eric Blair picked up his handset and radioed that he was on his way.

When Blair arrived on the scene, there was the usual complement of reporters, all screaming frantically into cell phones and trying to get inside. A second police cruiser pulled up simultaneously, and two officers set up a barrier across the street. Blair walked around to the back of the building, where smoke continued to billow lazily into the air. By the fence, what looked like an oversized ping pong table lay in several pieces on its side. A hole had been blown through one end, and there was a three-feet-deep crater in the ground.

Another policeman entered the yard and began to comb for evidence. Blair approached Charlie, who was sitting on the back stoop. His white button-down shirt was streaked with dirt; his eyes were glazed, his lashes singed.

"You all right?" Blair asked.

Charlie nodded, staring at the place where his model once stood.

"Then would you mind explaining what the hell is going on?"

CITY UNPLUGGED

LOUIS NAVARO HAD AN APPOINTMENT WITH THE TICKER doctor in Torrance at one, so he decided to pay a surprise morning visit to the home of his handyman, with the intention of finding out if the guy was truly a lousy worker or just in the habit of drinking early. Navaro could forgive the man his mediocrity, could forgive even his *own* mediocrity, but a drunk was a drunk was a drunk.

The handyman lived on Las Palmas Avenue, north of Hollywood Boulevard—in the land of malt liquor and crack smoke, of struggling guitar players and cold beans eaten from from cans. Navaro had planned only to drop in, say hello to the guy and check him out, then hop right on the 101 and pick up the 405 down to Torrance. At ten o'clock, though, the handyman didn't answer his door, so Navaro decided he'd walk around the neighborhood to see how it had changed.

He didn't get far. Hollywood Boulevard was closed to pedestrian and vehicular traffic from Highland to Fairfax. Proprietors of seedy establishments stood on sidewalks, arms folded, incensed; the tourists had no way to get to those T-shirts and fuzzy dice and postcard racks. At a street corner, as Navaro hit the change-light-please button, a policeman stopped him with his arm.

"Closed off. Sorry." In his other hand the cop held a Mag-Lite like a billy club.

"What's going on?"

"Making a movie." The cop sounded like he was directing it. "Warners. Earthquake picture. Big one."

Navaro sighed, then noticed a guy behind the barrier—a familiar face. The guy wore a black linen suit and spoke on a cellular phone. Navaro squinted, and it came to him.

"Hey! Ian!"

"OK, fella!" The cop held out his flashlight.

"I know that guy," Navaro told him.

"Yeah, an' Bridge Bridges is my brother."

"Hey!" Navaro called again.

Ian looked at him, blinked, and scurried into a trailer.

"Kid used to live in my building." Navaro turned and walked away. "I hope he chokes on his vomit."

Navaro didn't remember getting onto the 101, nor could he recall the fifteen-minute drive north to the 405 interchange. He'd made the trip before, and there was no mystery in it. Besides, he'd been rebuffed by this kid, Ian, and in his current state of mind that didn't help things. He'd misjudged the little sonuvabitch. He should have been nicer, but how the hell could he have known? "The kid scratches his belly all day and ends up a millionaire," he said aloud. Then he cut off a Toyota Corolla.

Navaro's reverie was interrupted when he reached the 405 and found it closed. He was irked further to see other drivers continuing north on the 101, forewarned by huge flashing arrows and detour markers to use an alternate route. Lost in thought, Navaro alone had not seen the signs.

He stopped his car, got out, and walked to a barrier where several dozen onlookers had assembled. From their conversation, he discerned that a movie was being shot, a truck was about to be blown up, and Bridge Bridges was on his way.

Suddenly, as the crowd watched, a helicopter began its descent. Wind from its propellers ripped through everyone's hair, and some people covered their faces with their arms. The helicopter landed, and even Navaro joined in the applause when Bridge Bridges emerged. Behind the actor were Henny Rarlin and, still talking on his cellular phone, Ian Marcus. Navaro rubbed his eyes.

Just an hour ago, moments before he'd seen Navaro on Hollywood Boulevard, Ian had been approached by an officious looking man in a Dragnet suit who'd handed him a summons. When he saw the words "Theft of Intellectual Property," Ian understood that Jon Kravitz, his erstwhile friend and collaborator, was suing him. Reading further, he found that unless he properly compensated this Jon Kravitz, *Ear to the Ground* could be enjoined. Bob Semel had called him immediately, and so had Michael Lipman—from his new corner office at ICM. Nothing yet from Ethan. Dr. Ehrich Weiss had come to his trailer wondering if he wanted to talk. Even Grace had been almost sweet to him. His lawyer was on his way to the set. Things were bad, and Ian was scared. There would be depositions taken. Depositions!

His father would fly out. Or he would go home and lie in bed for a week. Maybe Grace would take him back. Maybe she'd be surprised by the change in him. Through such a humbling experience, he'd learn integrity, and that's not such a bad thing.

Henny Rarlin grabbed Ian's arm. "We need a line for when the truck is going down and they're about to die."

"But I thought …"

"Yeah, but now we need a *line*."

Ian thought a moment.

"What do you think about 'fuck?'"

"Fuck? Why 'fuck?'"

"Homage to *Butch Cassidy*. Ironic because we one-up them language-wise, and then switch the result. Cassidy and Sundance live. These guys don't."

Henny Rarlin walked away from him. "Fuck *you*," he said. "I'll do it myself."

POINT OF ORIGIN

CHARLIE RICHTER WAS RUNNING OUT OF TIME. WITH THE earthquake only five weeks away, he began dreaming of crumbling cityscapes, of concrete walls and freeway overpasses reduced to dust. He sat rigidly at his desk, working for hours without moving. And around his shoulders, near the top of his spine, he developed a terrible knot.

Twice last week, he had tried to explain the concept of retroshocks to Caruthers, but both times he'd been dismissed by the man's jokes. "What are you blowing up next?" his boss asked him. "Anything *good*?"

Caruthers's reaction galled him because the retroshock idea was simple: Aim one force directly at another force of equal size and the two forces will be neutralized. What wasn't so simple was the question of magnitude, 8.9. About five thousand times the size of the Oklahoma City blast.

It wasn't long, however, before Charlie had a realization that was startling in its completeness, overwhelming in its immediate practical value. Like most great discoveries, it didn't come about by calculation, but rather by calculation's opposite.

Charlie was meditating, lying on his back with his knees slightly raised. He closed his eyes, and what he found behind his lids was not darkness at all, but an entirely different kind of light. When he stretched out his arms, he had the sensation of leaving his body and looking down from above. He was seized by an image, remembered from a snapshot, of his mother holding him as a baby, and unconsciously he curled into the fetal position. He felt confined, and a great pressure built up in his ears. Then the pressure ceased, and Charlie felt suddenly pure—pure, and clean, and newly born.

He got up and went to his desk, thinking about *birth*. Birth. Birth. Birth. Slowly, he began to smile.

Earthquakes worked in three stages, Charlie thought: beginning, middle, and end. It is the *end* we feel, the end that is tragic and destructive. In the end, the earth moves— after the offending energy, having been propelled across the planet, gathering steam under the surface, settles finally on its place of impact: the epicenter. At the beginning, however, there is a mere spark, whose damage comes only from what it can incite.

All along, Charlie had understood the way one temblor presaged another, fields of energy rippling back and forth across the Pacific plate like dominoes in a chain. He had used this information to predict the coming San Andreas quake, and to locate and project the epicenter at position D-55. Now the expression "Nip it in the bud" suggested itself to him.

He returned to his work table and began to manipulate data: magnitudes, longitudes and latitudes, dates and times and distance and miles. Via modem, he imported more data from the CES network, to pinpoint the exact time and place tectonic energy would begin to roll eastward toward Los Angeles. He looked at release histories and at projected points of origin from the San Francisco earthquake of 1906. Ditto Tokyo, 1923; Long Beach, 1933; and Anchorage, 1964. He pulled figures from Loma Prieta, Northridge, and Kobe, and soon he was swimming in his familiar sea of numbers. As the sun started to rise over the Los Angeles basin, he found a point near the island of Lui, an uninhabited member of the Hawaiian chain.

Charlie heard the slap of the *Los Angeles Times* against his front door. Outside, morning dew had become mist, and birds chirped more sweetly than usual. There was something lovely in their singing, some quality of hope Charlie had never before noticed. For the first time in a long time, he could see past December 29.

Charlie reached into his box to retrieve yesterday's mail. Among the bills and direct mail solicitations, he found a padded envelope embossed with the White House seal. Curiously, he tore it open and pulled out three Grateful Dead concert tapes and a short, handwritten note on presidential stationery.

Back inside, Charlie unfolded the newspaper and realized it was Thanksgiving. He slipped one of the Dead bootlegs into his tape deck, then pulled a chair in front of the television. After finding the Macy's parade, he turned the sound off. It had been a long time since he'd watched all those huge helium balloons float down Central Park West, but this morning his heart soared at the sight of them, drifting toward him above the latticework of Jerry Garcia's guitar.

He turned up the volume on the stereo and scrunched down into his seat. "Thank you," he said to no one in particular, eyes fixed on the screen.

DARKNESS VISIBLE

ON THURSDAY MORNING, THREE FIRST-UNIT FILM CREWS and six second units were splayed throughout the streets and establishments of greater Los Angeles. Principal photography on *Ear to the Ground*, more grueling than Ugandan boot camp, would end Monday at midnight—if all went well.

The day's excitement began with a scene—a *shot* really—where the camera was simply meant to record Bridge Bridges looking out the second-floor window of a crumbling apartment building in Northridge. Why it took so long to set up was anyone's guess. In the finished film, the image would precede the "WHAT-HE-SEES" shot, of a child crying in an adjacent window, which had been filmed two weeks earlier.

Bridge, deep in character and annoyed at having to stand around so long, had the impulse, on the second take, to bound from his window onto the trunk of a coconut palm he'd been watching sway gently for nearly an hour. He sprained his ankle.

At the same time, at the "B-Set" in the San Bernardino desert, ninety halogen lamps were being prepped to ignite in a flash near what would be the great quake's epicenter. The effect would last half a second onscreen, cost ninety thousand dollars, and hopefully inject a spiritual angle into the latter part of the story.

The wrinkle began at the "C-Set" downtown, at five o'clock, when a vehicle from the sheriff's office pulled up in front of the unit production manager's trailer. A deputy got out and knocked on the trailer door. He was told by a harried-looking girl that the UPM was currently on-set, and the girl began giving him directions.

"Just get him over here for me."

Fifteen minutes later, setups had ceased and cameras had stopped rolling in all three locations. Deputies held sway over their operations. No explanation was given.

It had been a shrewd decision on the part of Jon Kravitz and his lawyers to wait before they went after Warner Brothers. Now they could name their price. Ten million dollars had been their first demand, to test the waters in the sea of negotiation.

Consensus had been reached that Ian *had* spoken to Jon about *Ear to the Ground*. Jon's ideas had found their way into the script, and some of his bits had been committed to celluloid.

But Bob Semel and Ethan Carson were in agreement: Warner Brothers had bought from Ian Marcus what they assumed was his to sell. They owed nothing further, they felt, to either party. Michael Lipman, Ian's literary representative, denied everything and refused to relinquish any commissions.

Interested parties had assembled in the Warner's eighth-floor suite at the Four Seasons Hotel. Ian's lawyer was talking to Jon Kravitz's lawyer, or, rather, listening to him; Bob Semel and Ethan were on separate phones. Henny Rarlin showed up briefly with a girl on his arm, not his wife. Grace stopped by, and so did Dr. Ehrich Weiss, who assumed the air of a priest giving last rites.

Ian sat outside on the balcony, thinking about how fucked up life was, and how ridiculous it was to try to understand it. He really wanted a blended margarita more than anything, but worried that it was inappropriate. His feet were up on the railing, and he could feel lines forming around his eyes. How could this be happening?

Again, he did the math. Tax and commissions. The expenditures: first-class airline tickets, hotels, lunches to impress friends, tips out the wazoo, little things that catch the eye in boutique windows, taxis (just put your hand in the air!), the bottles of French wine he now took to dinner parties, the Mercedes, the fresh-water aquarium, the linen suits and silk shirts and socks that cost twelve dollars a pair, the beautiful bags of Humboldt green, and, of course, the incidentals: "Champagne, waiter!" Or, "Let's go to Vegas!"

Ehrich Weiss poked his head onto the balcony. "How are you?" he asked.

"Bad."

"Life goes on. It's not the end of the world."

Ian stared into space.

The doctor waited a moment. "Somebody wants to see you," he said, and disappeared.

Grace, Ian thought. It would have to be. She had always been attracted to his heartache, and Ian suspected she would be there in his darkest hour. She was dependable, if a bit tight around the lips. She meant well, and he guessed he loved her. Would always love her. Grace.

A moment later, Jon Kravitz came onto the balcony.

"Hey, man," he said. Ian couldn't look at him, and it took a moment to realize what was going on. Jon continued: "Just wanted to say it's not a personal thing. It's business. And I hope it doesn't put a permanent damper on our friendship."

"What?"

"It'll probably be a while before we have the kind of trust we once did. Just wanted to say if there's anything I can do ..." He nodded, and went inside.

Ian put his head in his hands. Then he got up, opened the door to the suite, and went to inspect the minibar.

BUYER'S MARKET

AT 4:15 ON THURSDAY AFTERNOON, THE HORSE AND BUGGY, a workingman's bar on Roscoe Boulevard in Northridge, was empty except for an elderly man drinking alone, a couple of kids from CSUN, and Henry Grant. He sat in the shadows, sipping a beer and talking to Eddie, the bartender, with whom he had a long, though glancing, acquaintance.

"Mike Blowers?" Henry was saying. "I wouldn't trade my *mother-in-law* for Mike Blowers."

"Your mother-in-law's dead, Henry."

"Thank Christ. She still plays a better third base."

Eddie looked down and took a swipe at the bar's burnished surface with a wet rag. "Come on, Henry. Two weeks, there ain't gonna be any Dodgers. No Dodger Stadium."

"That earthquake's never gonna happen."

"No?" Eddie gestured at the empty room. "Then where *is* everybody? Take a look outside. You ever see so many moving vans in your life?"

"Yeah, yeah, yeah." Henry waved him off. "All my neighbors are moving away ..."

"That doesn't worry you?"

Henry took a long pull off his beer. "Where the hell am I gonna go?"

Emma was sitting in the living room, watching Ricki Lake interview earthquake survivors about stress, when the doorbell rang. On her way to answer it, she glanced toward the backyard, where Dorothy was running in and out of her playhouse.

A short, stocky man in a business suit stood on the front steps. He clutched a peeling leather briefcase.

"Mrs. Grant?" he asked, and offered her a card. "Frank Baum, American Realty Company. Like to talk to you about your home."

"My husband isn't here." Emma regretted the words as soon as she'd said them. How stupid she must sound, like a child, unable to make a decision on her own. "I guess it'd be OK for a minute," she amended.

Inside, they sat around the kitchen table.

"You've owned this place how long?" he asked.

"About thirty years. It was my parents' house."

"Like to sell it?"

Emma didn't know how to answer. From the corner of her eye, she caught a glimpse of the backyard—of Dorothy tearing up her playhouse with glee. She envied her daughter's innocence, until she remembered the last quake, when the ceiling had collapsed and the little girl's arm had snapped like a twig. *Sell* the fucking house, she thought.

"I might," Emma said.

"Like to sell it *today*?"

"Today?"

"Your neighbors are gone."

"Not this minute. I don't think I can."

"When?"

"I don't know."

"Correct me if I'm wrong. I just heard you say you wanted to sell it."

"Well, I …"

"Why not now?"

Emma stood up and began rummaging for a coffee filter. "Would you like a cup of coffee?" she asked.

"Thanks," Baum said.

She turned on the tap and began measuring out the water, a gesture so ingrained it took no thought. Thirty years in this kitchen. Thirty years. As she poured in the grounds, she couldn't help considering another little girl, who bore her own name and face. She thought of her mother telling her a bedtime story in the room where her daughter now slept; and her father, in dirty work clothes, sipping beer and watching the Dodgers on television. The memories were like little films to her. And if she left this house, they would stay behind.

"I don't know what I want to do," she said.

Baum smiled. "Where did your next door neighbors go?"

"Tucson."

"I have a nephew in Tucson. In construction."

"My husband's in construction."

"Yeah?" Baum took a sip of his coffee. "My nephew's doing very well. Your husband should give him a call."

"I should talk it over with him first."

"Why? You own this house, don't you, Mrs. Grant?"

"How do you know that?"

Baum gave her a teasing smile and went to his briefcase. Two chrome latches slapped against the leather. He withdrew a piece of paper and placed it on the table in front of her.

"OK, Mrs. Grant," he said. "This is a bill of sale. One house at 1939 Topeka Drive, in exchange for a cashier's check in the sum of twenty thousand dollars."

"I ..."

"You want to sell this house, Mrs. Grant. Your neighbors have all moved away." He leaned in close across the table. "And your child was hurt in the last earthquake."

Emma felt the air explode from her lungs like someone had kicked her in the solar plexus. For a moment, she thought she was screaming, but then she looked around her and saw Baum nodding at her from across the table, while Dorothy continued to play in the backyard. The only sound was that of the kitchen faucet, dripping as it had for years.

Frank Baum took a check from his briefcase. Emma could make out her name, printed clearly, along with the dollar amount.

"This offer might not be available tomorrow," Baum said. "Tomorrow might be something else again." He pushed his gold pen across the table. "So, Mrs. Grant. What do you say?"

SEIZE THE DAY

IF CHARLIE RICHTER WANTED TO SAVE LOS ANGELES, HIS margin of error stood at less than one-tenth of a percent. Yet every time he thought seriously about his plan, he felt like he couldn't breathe.

On Tuesday night, Charlie would fly into Honolulu, where he would pick up plastic explosives before chartering a plane to the tiny island of Lui. There, he would use his rusty surveyor's skills to find the location his calculations had pinpointed: latitude 155.0357 degrees, longitude 19.8381. Two centuries earlier, a small volcano had anchored the spot, and Charlie hoped there were still some vestiges of rock and earth to mark it. If not, he thought, his face twitching into a grimace, I'm fucked. And so is L.A.

Charlie wished he didn't feel so isolated, but he was now, undeniably, on his own. CES was a joke, a mere arm of Warner Brothers, with Caruthers feeding information to the *Ear to the Ground* marketing machine. The CES director had grown so fond of the camera that he'd become a regular commentator on *Ricki Lake*, reassuring anxious citizens that a temblor was nothing to fear. He had allowed hype to overtake any sense of scientific responsibility, seduced by Hollywood into believing that seismologists were fortune tellers and the study of earthquakes nothing but a parlor game.

The whole thing made Charlie wonder if the City of Angels was worth saving, or if it was more noble to let it be destroyed. Then he looked out his window and saw two kids playing across the street. One wore an oversized flannel shirt so large it came down below his knees. At that moment, Charlie realized that, no matter what else happened, he had no choice but to try.

Grace Gonglewski hated spending Saturday morning on the phone, but she'd allowed Bob Semel's promises of money and power to overwhelm her better judgment. Having tripled Grace's salary, the president of the studio seemed convinced he owned a piece of her soul. At least that's what he'd told her at 7 a.m., when he called for his daily status report.

Grace had seen the ad in the *Los Angeles Times*. A full page in the Calendar section, featuring a photo of a crowded downtown L.A., split down the middle by the slogan: "Get Out Before It's Too Late!" As she twirled a strand of hair around her finger and waited on hold with Ethan Carson, Grace thought how appropriate that tag line truly was. With *Ear to the Ground* opening in three days, five hundred prints were said to be faulty and in need of recall. Bob Semel wanted answers, and the theater owners were going wild. Last night, Grace dreamt of empty movie screens and crowds rioting on Hollywood Boulevard in front of Mann's Chinese.

Fuck it, she thought, and lit a cigarette. Lately, she'd felt like writing again, felt scenes begin to articulate themselves slowly in her head. Partly, she guessed, it was due to Ian's success; partly the fact that she lived each day like a rubber band stretched to the breaking point.

This time, however, she wasn't thinking about writing a script—the fragments she jotted down were prose. She hadn't told anyone about it, not even Charlie, and she wasn't sure if it was delusion, or something that would one day take shape. But as she puffed on her cigarette, she could feel whatever it was starting to grow.

Charlie sat back in his chair and knitted his hands behind his head. Next to the computer, his recorder stood like a wooden sentry, fingerholes straight as coat buttons, mouthpiece a small, impassive head. How long had it been since he'd played? When he picked up the instrument and started to blow, its reedy tone was mournful as a Santa Ana wind.

The sound brought back the afternoon he had performed for Grace. The music was high and clear and full of hope: a sweet madrigal evoking the sustaining power of love. Five and a half months ago, he thought. It might as well be centuries. He felt ancient now, as if the weight of everything was laid across his back. Lately, he'd noticed tiny lines around his eyes and had become convinced he was growing old before his time.

On the computer screen, a simulated image of Lui sent waves of energy out into the Pacific. As Charlie watched, he pictured himself there with Grace. It was just a flash, gone as quickly as it appeared. But it left behind a sliver of anticipation, and, for the second time that morning, the certainty that he should seize the day.

So Charlie put down his recorder and headed for the stairs. On the second-floor landing, he knocked at Grace's door. For an instant, there was no sound from within. Then the door swung open, revealing Grace, phone in the crook of her neck, looking as if she'd rather be anywhere else.

"Oh, hi," she said, eyes coming alive at the sight of his face. She waved him inside, and mumbled a hurried goodbye into the phone.

"Hi," Charlie said, and took a step toward her. "I think we need to talk."

WAITING FOR THE
END OF THE WORLD

ON TUESDAY, DECEMBER 26, THE UNITED STATES ARMY sent double-rotored helicopters into the Los Angeles basin to monitor distress. Throughout the Southland, it was as if Christmas had never happened. In its place was an eastward stream of packed station wagons and moving vans that had now become a deluge. An ordinance had made it illegal for employers to penalize workers for leaving town and, as a result, most businesses were closed until after the first of the year.

Virtually everything had been affected by the coming disaster—and every corner of the nation's second largest metropolitan area experienced this psychic foreshock. It was in such an atmosphere that Warner Brothers opened its $210 million extravaganza *Ear to the Ground.*

At the premiere, Bruce Springsteen's "Shaken Up" played softly in the courtyard at Mann's Chinese. Behind police barricades, throngs of rubberneckers and leaner-inners and know-they-can'ts reached for Henny Rarlin as he got out of his limousine with an unidentified woman—not his wife—and assumed a camera smile. A lot was on Henny's mind. This fucking movie could kill him. It could send him to the minor leagues, or worse: Finland, to make documentaries on Laplanders. Henny had been drinking since noon, and as he strode cotton-mouthed down the red carpet, he thought only of reaching his seat without incident.

Another limousine yielded Ethan Carson with Sandra Bullet, who broke her heel as she got out, and recovered marvelously by enacting a Chaplinesque pantomime, in which she attempted to hide her imperfections from the fans. Sandy hoped her cameo as the seismologist's wife would alter the lovable-but-slightly-naive-girl image she'd acquired. As flashes went off around them, Ethan spent his energy considering whether people would actually think he and Sandy were an item.

Grace came with—she had to laugh—Matt Dillinger, who was exactly like the character he portrayed in *Lasso the Pharmacist*. As a fireman in *Ear to the Ground*, he repeatedly risked his life, always emerging sweaty and covered with soot. Grace wanted to come alone, but that was vetoed by Ethan. "What about your seismologist?" he asked her, mentally tallying the publicity Charlie's presence might generate. "Out of town," she'd said, and suggested Dillinger.

Ian couldn't have guessed they would boo him. He'd thought, given the circumstances, the applause might be strange, maybe meager, maybe even nonexistent. But, as the third-from-last title—"Written by Ian Marcus"—faded up, the catcalls began.

Ian sunk down in his seat and looked around for his date. Her name was Maria, and she was very pretty, but she was nowhere to be found. The Jon Kravitz lawsuit had made page one in *Variety* for a full week, and Ian was now notorious in the town that had once ignored him. Listening to the tumult, he wished silently for some kind of reprieve. Then, to hide his identity, he began to boo along with the crowd.

Grace had seen the film plenty of times, so she relaxed and let herself drift. Almost immediately, Charlie's image came to mind. Grace could hardly remember his face, but she could see his chest clearly, with its strawberry tuft of hair. She liked that chest, and she remembered being surprised when Charlie had taken off his shirt and propped it on her bedpost. Quite surprised.

The movie was predictable but entertaining. Special effects—especially sound effects—were tremendous. At the climax, as the earthquake hit and walls tumbled in on an audience watching a movie about an earthquake, the effect was suitably disturbing. So much so that, when the lights came up, those Hollywood luminaries remembered it *wasn't* just a movie.

For this reason, an un-native hue of resolution fell over the afterparty.

People drank less than usual, but smoked more cigarettes and pot, which entailed walking to the far end of the soundstage and cramming onto a sliver of patio. It got so popular out there that the caterers peeled the tent back as much as possible without causing it to collapse on itself.

Bob Semel sat near the bandstand with his division heads, projecting grosses. Reviews were only a minor consideration, but if the earthquake was a dud, they were in deep shit. This picture should have opened a month ago, and Semel knew it. Now all he could do was airlift the studio to Tucson, Arizona, and hope for the worst.

Around the room, the talk was earthquake, earthquake, earthquake. "Look for a slew of movies about 'em," Sterling Caruthers told a pair of actresses.

"You a producer?" a bobbed redhead asked him.

"Among other things, yes. I helped produce this film."

"Really?" the other one asked.

"I'm director of the Center for Earthquake Studies."

"A producer *and* a director!" The redhead made a joke.

"The truth is"—Caruthers took her hand—"I like the *movies*. I just signed with Warners to consult on scientific matters, with a first-look deal on projects of my own."

"*Exciting!*" the redhead said.

"Listen," Caruthers continued, "I'm leaving in five minutes, and thought you might like to come with me."

"Uh ... where?"

"To a press conference, briefly. Then, hopefully, to a nice supper."

The redhead looked over at her friend.

"I just need to leave, that's all," Caruthers said, and smiled gently.

"Sure," she looked back at him. "That sounds fun."

Charlie Richter sat in a cab driving down La Cienega toward LAX. Beside him on the back seat was a rucksack containing some clothes, a laptop computer, a surveyor's compass, and nasty-looking drill bits designed to cut through volcanic rock. In his hand, he held the photo of Grace he'd stolen so many months ago, her face as unreadable as the first time he'd seen it.

Charlie didn't regret telling Grace about the retroshock, nor about the trip to Lui. He also didn't regret what happened after they'd finished talking, although it had complicated things. Now, on his way out of town, he felt as if he were leaving a little piece of himself behind. For the first time since he was a boy, he felt like Los Angeles was home. At the same time, he was more than a little worried: L.A. could become a very dangerous place in the next few days.

The cab's AM radio spilled a litany of panic into the air. Every flight out of LAX, Burbank, Ontario, and John Wayne had been booked through Thursday night, and all four airports would be closed on December 29. It was impossible to find a seat anywhere—even on a bus or a train. The freeways, too, were overloaded: If you took the 10 east from La Cienega, it would take two hours to reach downtown. All across Southern California, entire neighborhoods had become modern ghost towns. There were isolated reports of looting, and clusters of small fires dotted the night sky.

At the airport, the gridlock was impossible. So Charlie paid the driver and walked around the terminal buildings until he found Hawaiian Air. Wherever he looked, young men and women in white robes walked in wide circles, chanting and holding up signs: "The End Is Near" and "Welcome to the Apocalypse."

Charlie had heard about these people, these apocalyptics, who, in the last week or so, had actually begun *arriving* in L.A. And who knows: they could be *right*. But Charlie knew, if everything worked out as planned, they would once again be denied the chance to glimpse the face of God. It was not his intention to interfere with their faith but, in the end, faith was such a tenuous thing. Charlie's was in the perfectibility of science, the way everything, if examined properly, could be codified and explained.

At a quarter to seven on Wednesday morning, the sun was barely a rumor, daylight gray and streaked with purple, silent but for a tentatively squawking bird. In the driveway of 1939 Topeka Drive, Emma Grant stood wiping her hands on her sweatpants, staring at the house.

It had all happened so quickly. One minute, she'd been sitting at the kitchen table, staring at the bill of sale; the next, Henry was standing over her, transfixed by the sight of that twenty-thousand-dollar check. She hadn't heard him come in, but Frank Baum sure had, and within half an hour, the paperwork had been signed, the money turned over, and Henry was talking, talking—always talking—about how they were rich.

Emma shook her head. Twenty thousand dollars. It wouldn't last long, she thought. And yet twenty thousand dollars was what her whole life was worth. She'd walked through every room in the house that night, trying to memorize the details of her past. But as soon as they took the check, the past started to dissipate. Standing here now, it was hard for her to remember anything but their decision to leave.

Henry came out the front door carrying two suitcases, which he threw in the back of his pickup. The truck bed was stuffed to the point of bulging; throw in anything else, Emma thought, and the suspension would give way.

"That's it," Henry said, and lit a cigarette. The smoke was invisible against the early morning sky. "All set?"

Emma nodded. Henry acted as if they were merely going for a spin. She looked up and down Topeka Drive and saw a forest of "Sold" signs. Last night, she passed the park where Dorothy played. The trees had been uprooted, and a team of FEMA workers were frantically constructing a tent city on the newly cleared land. It was so much like January 1994 that she pulled the car over to catch her breath.

When she got home, she had begun packing immediately, losing herself in an attempt to forget. The news contained reports of more looting, and Emma felt tears welling in her eyes. She had ridden her bike on this street, and watched her daughter do the same. She wondered if they'd ever come back to this place, and if they did, what would remain. Would the ordered pattern of houses and streets survive, or would they all be shaken away?

Henry went around to the pickup's cab and climbed inside. After a moment, the tinny voice of a traffic reporter alerted them that the 405 was backed up all the way from the 101 to the 5. Henry took a drag off his cigarette and squinted at the sky.

"It's getting late," he said. "Why don't you wake the little girl?"

In Honolulu, Charlie met a leathery-faced man who sold him sixty pounds of plastic explosives—enough to sink a battleship. Then he chartered an amphibious plane that could land in the small natural harbor of Lui and coast toward the shore. Fifty yards from the island, he lowered an inflatable raft into the warm Pacific waters, threw down his gear, and told the pilot when to pick him up on Thursday. Then the plane took off, and Charlie realized he was utterly alone.

On the beach, Charlie took inventory: food, water, flashlight, drill, generator, laptop, and explosives. He began to trek inland. The ground was hilly, with outcroppings of volcanic rock rising in irregular formations, and lush, overhanging growth so dense it obscured the sun. Humidity made the whole place feel like a sauna, and before he'd gone half a mile, Charlie stripped down to his underwear. Grace's presence, like an invisible spirit, hovered at his hand, and he imagined what it would be like if she were there, running naked with him in and out of the sea.

But there would be plenty of time for vacations. Briefly, he was struck by the old familiar doubts—that what he was trying to do was absurd, a small man's attempt to tamper with the forces of nature. Then Grace's face returned to him. She was in Los Angeles, he thought, and he appreciated the fact that it meant he had no choice but to succeed.

Eventually, Charlie came to a clearing with a dusty covering of brittle soil. This is it, he thought. He checked his compass and the coordinates of his map. His stomach began to flutter, accompanied by a clenching of his sphincter and a tightening of his balls. To his right, like a revelation, was the shape of a small, dormant volcano, its rocky sides rising in jagged minarets to the sky.

Charlie threw off his backpack and took out his equipment piece by piece. He turned on the laptop, and an image of Lui appeared on the screen, along with specific coordinates, angles of entry, and depths of charge.

He spent a while comparing the computer simulation with the actual landscape, walking off distances and doing tests of the soil. On the southwest side of the volcano, Charlie went to work. The drill whined like a dentist's, its three diamond-tipped bits glinting in the sun like bad teeth. He looked at his watch. Wednesday, December 27, three-seventeen p.m. Less than twenty-nine hours to go.

Thursday morning, Grace was awakened at six-thirty by the phone. She had been dreaming of Charlie, and when the ringing sliced its way into her consciousness, her first thought was that he was dead. When she got to the living room, however, it was Ian's voice emerging from the answering machine, plaintive and petulant.

"Come on, Grace," he was saying. "I know you're there."

She turned the volume down, but the damage was done. Back in bed, she couldn't sleep. Pictures swirled in her mind: Charlie trekking through the middle of nowhere, without sufficient food or water. With explosives strapped to his back. Charlie stumbling. Charlie falling.

Shit, Grace thought. She took off her nightgown, pulled on a pair of jeans, and caught a glimpse through the open window of the sun rising in the east. The sky was clear as ice; the flanks of the mountains stained rose with spreading light. Tomorrow, she thought, it could all be gone.

Grace walked up Spaulding toward Melrose, listening for even the slightest sign of life. They were reporting violence, but here the street was deserted, with a single car parked at the curb. In the last few days, she had watched her neighbors leaving town, even as her life continued to be possessed by *Ear to the Ground*. I should call Semel, she thought. When I get back.

Nearly all the stores were shuttered on Melrose, strips of tape X-ed across windows as silent supplication to the gods, or protection against them. Cops stood at intersections, along with members of the National Guard. Grace was surprised to find the Martel Avenue newsstand open, and as she plunked down her fifty-four cents for the *Times* she wished the proprietor good luck. One section today, twelve pages, with no advertising and no sports or lifestyle sections. Just earthquake news.

When Grace returned home, Navaro was sitting on the front steps having a cigarette.

"Smoke?" he asked her, gesturing with his pack.

"I've got my own, thanks." She shook out a Merit, and accepted his offer of a light.

"I'm surprised you're still around," he said.

"What about you?"

"All I got's right here." Navaro waved loosely at the building. "Somebody has to protect it."

Grace almost laughed. "From who?"

"You watch the news? There's animals out there. Taking what ain't theirs." His mouth twisted into a snarl, and all of a sudden Grace could imagine what he must have looked like as a young man. It wasn't an altogether unattractive picture, and she found herself starting to get drawn in.

"Anybody tries to fuck with this place, they're gonna get a big surprise."

He leered at her conspiratorially, before letting his face settle back into a mask of stone. Grace could see him waiting, like a little boy, for her to ask what he had in mind. Give him his thrill, she thought, and smoked for a moment. "Surprise?"

"That's right," Navaro said. He raised himself up, and became an old man again before Grace's eyes. He put one hand on his chest and with the other fumbled with his jacket, removing something from the pocket that looked like a length of iron pipe. The sun glinted off the metal, and she had to squint. Then she recognized a barrel and a chamber, and she realized with a shock of horror that her landlord had a gun in his hand.

By six-forty-five Thursday evening, Charlie had drilled twenty-three one-inch-diameter holes in an octagonal pattern, all seventeen-and-seven-eights inches deep. Twenty-three detonator pins, one in each hole, had been lowered, and held in place with plastique—soft but heavy—and frightening to the touch. It would be the ultimate irony for Charlie to have come this far, and end up as nothing but a fine red mist.

He tried to work slowly, but he was falling behind. In an hour and nineteen minutes, an energy flow would trigger a spark that, unchecked, would sweep across the Pacific and detonate the San Andreas. Charlie couldn't shake the feeling that things would not be ready in time.

By seven-fifty-one, however, he had finished packing the explosives around the detonator pins and connecting it all to a single fuse. The fuse ran to a digital timer, which—after checking his calculations—Charlie set. By flashlight, he made a final check of his wiring, then stood and admired his work. It was an amazing thing, if you thought about it, that science had brought him here.

Charlie picked up his rucksack and started to run. It was a mile from the jungle back to the harbor. Every few minutes, he checked his watch, but time had become a fluid entity, no longer reliable in any way he could understand. Seconds felt like minutes, minutes like hours. Just a few hours earlier, the reverse had been true, and he wondered if that were also the case in Los Angeles, where the remaining citizens were struggling to prepare for whatever might come their way.

The thought startled him, and he stopped. For the first time, he began to wonder why he had not gone public with the retroshock idea. Los Angeles had been so disrupted—abandoned and dispirited; perhaps and, certainly, hopefully, none of it had been necessary at all. He stood there in the brush, regret palpable on his skin. "Shit," he said aloud. "I should have told them." A moment later, the explosives blew.

The blast was like a blitzkrieg. It hit with a percussive thwap that rattled Charlie's knees and a white burst of light that seared him to the spot. A second later, a hot wind came tearing through the jungle and knocked him to the ground. His head glanced off a piece of rock, and when he touched his brow, his fingers came away with blood.

Afterwards, the silence was the deepest Charlie had ever known. He tore a strip off his shirt and bandaged his head, then shouldered his pack and continued. The crystal on his watch was broken, and its hands had been fused into place by the heat. But Charlie knew he had done everything he could.

AND THE EARTH STOOD STILL

ON FRIDAY, DECEMBER 29, SEVENTEEN EARTHQUAKES disrupted the surface of the earth. The largest was a 3.3 that struck the Philippines, near Manila. In Los Angeles, the day looked like any other: hills standing in stark relief against valleys, ocean, and sky.

All afternoon, the city lay paralyzed by anticipation. People found themselves jumping at every rustle of wind, every barking dog, every creak and groan. As night began to fall, lights flickered in what few inhabited buildings remained, candles of faith against the darkness. It was like Christmas, but with utter lawlessness. An elderly man walking along La Cienega threw a brick through the front window of Ed Debevic's. Hoodlums got inside the Bank of America at Sunset and Vine but couldn't figure out where the money was.

In the parking lot outside the Center for Earthquake Studies, Sterling Caruthers sat on a temporary dais, before three hundred journalists, waiting for the ground to move. As the clock crept toward midnight, he found himself reverting to a childhood habit—prayer. Please, he thought, let it come *now*. And when nothing happened, he thought again: Now. Now. Now.

At twelve-oh-three a.m., Caruthers felt compelled to take the microphone. "The earth is an inconsistent conductor of seismic energy," he said. "Our simulations of the past few days indicated we might be running late."

"Why didn't you tell us before?" somebody bellowed. Similar questions came from all around him.

Caruthers fired back. "Think this is a *game*?" The crowd grew silent. "You think this is fun? This doom?" He slammed his fist against the podium, playing the outraged elder statesman. Actually, he had been hoping the quake would be delayed, knowing his power would increase exponentially until New Year's. At that point, in the absence of seismic activity, he'd be run out of town on a rail.

From Honolulu, Charlie left a message on Grace's machine— that everything had gone more or less as planned. Knowing he'd be unable to fly into L.A, he booked a flight to Phoenix instead and rented a car. He got home before midnight, and found a bottle of champagne in the fridge, a red rose, and a note:

Meeting going till late. See you after. You're my hero, baby. XO (love) Grace.

The bed had been turned down and sprinkled with rose petals, and Charlie's stomach fluttered at the thought of Grace being there while he was gone. He smelled her on his pillow, and the sense he got was one of home, of a life shared, complete. Her presence was like a bright light illuminating the empty corners of these rooms.

Charlie hopped in the shower. Ten minutes later, he was in his car, headed for CES. At twelve-twenty-nine a.m., he reached the parking lot and found thirty people standing in his space. News of Charlie's presence rippled through the crowd. The reporters turned en masse and barraged him with questions.

"Charlie Richter, ladies and gentlemen," Caruthers said, and reluctantly yielded the floor.

Charlie had saved the world, or at least part of the world. And he was in love. He knew, like few people ever know, that he'd reached the proverbial most important moment of his life. For a second, he saw white and heard in his mind's ear a sort of cymbal crash. Then he swallowed, and gripped the sides of the podium tightly. "The earthquake we expected this evening … has been averted," he mumbled, cotton-mouthed.

Before he had time to cough, the crowd went wild. Charlie cleared his throat and pulled a large sketchpad from his knapsack. "This is called a retroshock …"

Caruthers felt blood throbbing in his neck and suddenly wanted to be sick. "It isn't coming," Charlie continued, calmly. "The earthquake has been redirected. It's nothing to worry about …"

People finally shut up when Maggie Murphy from the *Los Angeles Reader* climbed atop a car and began screaming Charlie's name.

"Dr. Richter! Are you asking us to believe you just *stopped* the earthquake?" She seemed to shimmer like an angel, her black hair shiny under the fluorescent lights.

"Yes," Charlie said.

Then Murphy's eyes narrowed, her voice grew tight, and she wasn't an angel anymore. "You guys should be tarred and feathered," she said.

Caruthers's mind was whirling. He had only one option—to stand by Charlie. His *genius*. If the earthquake came, fine. If it didn't, at least the retroshock would provide some sort of *out*.

He put his arms around Charlie's shoulder, gave him a Hollywood hug, and leaned forward to speak. "We live in a world of science and hope for the future, where great —"

That was all he could get out before the crowd pressed in, sending both him and Charlie inside to the discredited halls of CES.

THE NUMBERS GAME, PART TWO

ETHAN CARSON'S HOUSE ON THE BEACH IN MALIBU HAD been decorated entirely in black, white, and gray. The idea, he'd been told by a designer, was to accentuate the *people* in the rooms. This made perfect sense, because Ethan entertained movie stars who were constantly in need of accentuation. Stockpiles of champagne lay in wait in the garage's auxiliary refrigerator. Whether that champagne would be brought out at all, or bourbon served instead, was a matter of the numbers.

People began dropping by his monochrome palace before noon, as Ethan was busy making calls to theater chains, plugging the data into a computer program called "MOVIEGROSS." By one o'clock, Henny Rarlin was on the veranda, already drunk. *Ear to the Ground* had made $37 million in its opening week, but it was uncertain whether the film would continue to do business—or, as the industry put it, "had legs." If, in the second weekend, grosses dropped by more than half, they were in big trouble. But if they dropped by, say, a quarter, they were in business. Big business.

The movie had opened on 2,900 screens on December 29, to mixed reviews. Janet Maslin of *The New York Times* called it a provocative concept with "Escheresque complexity," but she also said it was "uneven in tone." Gene Shalit, who loves everything, said it was the "scariest movie ever." Then again, Peter Travers, from *Rolling Stone*, referred to it as "history's most egregious waste of film stock." Matters were worsened by that day's *Chicago Tribune*, which ran a feature discussing the merits of capitalizing on disaster, indirectly accusing Warner Brothers of a bogus collusion with the Center for Earthquake Studies: "How Schlock Science Sells Seats."

The fact remained that no earthquake had come. And Ethan Carson didn't need MOVIEGROSS to spell it out: It was a crapshoot. In the absence of their "marketing earthquake," they had little chance of making money. Losing *less* became his mantra, and soon after Bridge Bridges had been made comfortable, Ethan poured his first bourbon.

Having slept until noon without any intention of stopping by Ethan's (he'd been invited out of necessity), Ian Marcus had a hankering for a Big Mac and Shake-'em-Up Shake. Mired in negativity and despair, he hadn't called anyone back for two weeks. His friends, he was certain, were abandoning him. Even his mother had asked him if he'd "copied off that other boy."

Still, Ian found solace seeing his name on various promotions connected with *Ear to the Ground*: in the newspaper, on billboards, television, and at McDonald's. "Written by Ian Marcus," it said, and it was true. How hard it was, though, to know where the ideas came from. If Ian thought back to that night at Damiano's, he still couldn't say whether Jon Kravitz had actually invented plot, or had simply led Ian to certain conclusions.

Ian drove to Mann's Chinese, showed the manager his Writers Guild card, and walked into an afternoon screening of *Ear to the Ground*. He watched without bias and, along with a highly excited audience, truly enjoyed the movie. Bridge Bridges was wonderful, he thought. The laughs were in all the right places, and there was even applause as the closing credits rolled.

Ian was hopeful again. He strolled down Hollywood Boulevard, along the Walk of Fame and, as he happened past Pearl Bailey's star, something came to him: "The Lord giveth, and the Lord taketh away." Giveth and Taketh. He jumped into his car and raced home.

Funny how an idea comes like a seed. A seedling, an inspiration. By the time Ian reached his desk, he'd developed a protagonist and a story line. How simple it was: the man who'd lost everything. He lit a joint and, four hours later, had fourteen pages of a new screenplay.

At first, Ethan Carson thought the man from Landmark Theaters Dallas had miscalculated. He was certain that, instead of a weekend figure, the man was quoting for the entire week. Ethan immediately called someone in marketing at Warner Brothers and found that, indeed, they were doing serious business in Dallas. Ditto, Boston and Philadelphia, Seattle and Portland. Chicago had been slow Saturday afternoon, but had picked up, selling out its three o'clock matinees. New York held steady. The only competition was a film directed toward black women, *Holding It In*.

Ear to the Ground, it appeared, had legs a mile long. It didn't drop off at all, would do $36 million in its second week, for a "cume" of $73 million, and would likely do $550 million globally. Ethan became graceful and buoyant when he received Bob Semel at the door, and by six o'clock there were two hundred people at the Carson house, drinking enough champagne to float the *Queen Mary*.

PLAYING THE ODDS

HENRY GRANT HAD NO INTENTION OF MOVING TO TUCSON. He'd been there once, and it wasn't his kind of town. Emma talked about it like it was the Promised Land, but to Henry it was just a flat, ugly place where the bars closed early. He kept his mouth shut, though, until they reached the intersection of the 10 and the 15, where he took the road to Vegas.

"Think of it like a vacation," he told Emma, when she protested. "Dorothy'll love it."

Emma slid away from him, leaning up against her door so hard she had to press down the lock. "I'm sure that's exactly what you have in mind."

"It'll be fun," he said, and floored the pickup, trying to make a little time.

That night, after Emma and Dorothy were asleep in their cheap motel room, Henry took a drive down the Strip. The desert sky was dark, but the lights of Vegas sparkled against it like stars come to earth. In the lobby of the Mirage, dolphins swam and trees reached up to an artificial sky, and he thought what a kick Dorothy would get out of the place. Then Henry heard the ching-ching-ching of the casino, and left all sense of family behind.

He started with five dollar blackjack, where he found a seat at the center of the table, next to a postal worker from Kansas who was in the process of losing his rent. He won his first hand when the dealer went bust on a sixteen, and the second when he drew a twenty-one. Easy. By the time the blonde cocktail waitress—who was wearing a cheerleader's outfit—brought him his third free beer, Henry had seven hundred in winnings. So he decided on a bit of a challenge.

Henry had never really understood craps, but it seemed simple enough. Instead of cards, it was *dice*. Besides, it was where the action was. So he threw down a couple of hundred dollar chips, ordered a bourbon, and set about learning the ropes. A pretty redhead blew three times on the dice before she threw them, her diamond bracelet jangling and catching the light.

The game moved fast. Nickel come; nickel go. Play the field. Hardways. Make the number. Easy as pie. And by three AM, when his education had cost him two thousand dollars, he jumped in the pickup loaded with his family's possessions and went back to his motel room on tip-toes, for a little more tuition money.

He'd learned enough to know the odds were with the house, always with the house. But when he played "Don't Pass," the house suddenly got cold. Sick of pulling out a hundred here and a hundred there, he bought five grand worth of chips, thinking the stack would bring him confidence and luck. Besides, he would never bet it *all*. That was for suckers. When it was his turn to roll, he bet against himself, and, dumb luck, he rolled beautifully.

An hour later, Henry sat in a men's room stall and counted his money. Ten thousand was gone. He was drunk, his mouth dry. No more craps, he thought. He sat back against the wall. His heart fluttered, and he hoped it would attack him. "Die, Henry, die!" he murmured to himself. No such luck.

But after a while, back out at the bar, Henry had an inspiration. Or rather a conversation, with a middle-aged man, about how the 49ers—who would face the Green

Bay Packers in the playoffs the following day—couldn't lose. "Y'got the best coached organization in the history of professional sports," the man said. "And they got two other important things. The best offense in the league, and the best defense, too."

Yeah, Henry thought. The 49ers. The 49ers are a sure thing.

So on his way out of the casino at six-forty-five in the morning, Henry laid his money down. Ten thousand on the San Francisco 49ers. If he won, he'd break even. The spread was ten points, but the Niners always won big in the playoffs. And, points or no points, only a fool would bet Green Bay. He drove back to the motel and crept into bed.

Six hours later, at the end of the first quarter, the score was 14-0, Packers.

"Why do we have to stay here and watch football?" Emma wanted to know.

"Yeah, why?" Dorothy chimed in.

"Go on out if you wanna go out!" Henry snapped.

When Green Bay marched down the field to make it 21-0, and the 49er faithful began booing their team, Henry knew it was too late. He threw the remote control at the television screen, smashing it into a dozen pieces.

"What's wrong with you, Henry?" Emma yelled. "It's only a game!"

And, trying unsuccessfully to clear his throat as her words echoed in his ears, Henry readied himself for a life of desperation and pain.

END OF THE ROAD

STERLING CARUTHERS GOT INTO HIS CAR AND SAT FOR A moment. He looked through the windshield, the way people do when they're not thinking about anything specific, or really anything at all. He was staring at the hedges that separated his Laurel Canyon home from that of his neighbor, a man who played catcher for the Dodgers, and with whom, until recently, he was on friendly terms.

Caruthers backed carefully out of his driveway, ran a stop sign at the bottom of his street, and six minutes later was moving northwest in medium traffic on the 101. It was not yet seven a.m., and he consoled himself with the knowledge that the sun was tormenting drivers in the opposite direction. The weather was fair, but the San Fernando Valley was bleak somehow, crawling with cars like maggots on a mango. If he craned his neck, Caruthers could see Warner Brothers, with its soundstages, its bungalows, its trailers and little golf carts, that dreadful commissary, and those corporate offices where he'd been lattéd and seltzered endlessly. He'd like to blow the whole studio up. Maybe he'd get away in time and maybe not. What did it matter, anyway?

As he passed the exit for Calabasas, which he'd taken too often to go to the home of his ex-wife's parents, he wondered if the force of the Warner explosion would take care of them, too. The whole family had turned on him when they'd learned of one of his extramarital affairs. A minor indiscretion: It had been meaningless, drunken, nothing compared with his love for Emily.

Still, it had gone on for more than a year. Those same in-laws had been so warm before—he often enjoyed golf with Emily's father, who called him "Ster," or sometimes "son."

"Two birds with one bomb," he thought, enamored of the phrase. Then he realized a bomb in Burbank would never blow in Calabasas. Caruthers recognized a pattern: They'd abandoned him, like everybody did. Two wives had left him, a poor one he loved and a rich one he didn't. He regretted losing them both. He tried to remember their faces, but could only remember photographs of their faces. Though his second wife wore Chanel, he could conjure only the *idea*, and not the smell of the perfume. He remembered the dress—black polka-dots on white—one of his mistresses wore like a bathrobe, after they'd had sex. Made love. He couldn't imagine her *wearing* the dress; he could only see it hanging there, up on the end of a door.

The fuel reserve light had been on for fifteen minutes, so Caruthers pulled his 1967 Rolls-Royce Corniche convertible into a Texaco station just off the freeway, and surprised the attendant at the Full Service pumps by asking for only five dollars' worth of regular.

"Check under the hood?"

"No," he told the grease-covered man. "The oil is fine."

He got back on the 101 and reached the place where buildings ended and those sprawling cypress trees seemed tiny on the hilltops. He took the Los Virgenes exit and eventually reached Malibu Canyon Road.

The sight of red rock all around him was awesome; the massive slabs sprawled underneath as he climbed the final straightaway through the mountains. Soon, like a flash, that two-mile canyon stretch would afford him his first glorious sight of the Pacific Ocean, only to yank it away like a bullfighter's cape as the car rounded another curve. Caruthers thought how life did that: dangle fruit so you could smell its ripeness, then snatch it away.

No good lawyer would represent him, and prosecutors had even discussed charging him with treason. The Center for Earthquake Studies was finished, padlocked, under investigation. It had been a good idea, Caruthers thought. It had almost worked.

It's not too difficult to lose control of a car if that's what you're after. Caruthers had read it in a book: At a fairly high speed, with an automatic transmission, simply shift into "Neutral" and then jam it into "Reverse." The gears won't catch, but they'll almost certainly jam, and the car will change speed at a rate so unpredictable that you're sure to do something strange to compensate. In Caruthers's case, the car veered sharply to the right. To compensate he turned left, but *too far* left. At eighty miles per hour, this sent him easily through the guardrail, and the convertible went sailing through the air. If you were close by in Malibu Canyon early that morning, you'd have thought that his car would fly.

Caruthers's last thought interested him: Life is a takeoff and a landing, with turbulence in between. Two seconds later, the car crashed—headlights first, and rolled once, end over end. Then, instead of exploding, the five dollars' worth of regular began to burn very slowly.

HAPPILY EVER AFTER

GRACE GONGLEWSKI HAD NEVER HIRED A MOVING company before. All her college moves, along with the one across the country, had been of the lug-it-yourself variety: truck rental, hunting for empty boxes, and friends who could be lured by pizza and beer.

This time, however, she and Charlie decided to relax and splurge. She'd made goodbye calls to three people; the others—that slew of acquaintances she'd acquired during four years in L.A.—could simply dial the Arizona number on the recording Pac Bell said they'd keep on her old number for ninety days.

Charlie hated moving. He couldn't stand the sight of movers bumping his delicate machines into the walls. Especially the lumino-oscilloscope, a one-of-a-kind device that measured minute thermal shifts in certain magna and strata. On moving days he always wished he were a blues singer, with nothing but the shirt on his back, able to walk into any bar, anywhere, and sing so well the owner would come out with a plate of steaming food, a glass of good red wine, and a key to the room upstairs. Charlie had moved many times, but this time things were different.

Their first fight had been about Charlie staying nearly every night at Grace's apartment, and how he'd come, unconsciously, to resent it. Grace told him she was more than happy to stay at his place, but four days later they were both sick of the spartan, bachelor-y way Charlie had arranged his possessions. Finally, they decided to find a place *together*. This conclusion, along with certain others, was reached over a romantic meal at Cafe des Artistes, where Grace had ordered a second bottle of wine because—though you could never know what was going to happen—it was still possible to look across a table and think you were seeing the rest of your life. For a moment, while she smiled into Charlie's eyes, a reddish light radiated behind his head and the rest of the room went dark.

On their last night in Los Angeles, they made love on the carpet of her bedroom. The apartment was empty, hollow, and their voices ricocheted strangely through the rooms. They might have stayed in the living room—after all, the bed had been taken away—but they'd come to the bedroom almost by rote, or by fate, and they laughed when they realized this.

They awoke simultaneously in each other's arms; they showered together and, two distinct eloquences of economy, they finished their last-minute tasks with unprecedented swiftness.

"I'm selling the building." Navaro told them as they came down his path for the last time. "Was on the phone all morning."

"Wow," Grace said.

"Thing is …" Navaro looked serious. "Lemme ask you a question."

Charlie and Grace both leaned forward.

"I'm in a moral *quarry*."

Grace smiled at Navaro's mistake, and Charlie pinched her discreetly.

Navaro went on. "I think the *guy* thinks there's four apartments in the building. But he never saw it. Y'know?"

"You mean he doesn't know about the duplex?" Charlie asked.

Navaro shook his head. "But *you* liked it, din't ya?"

Charlie smiled. "Sure I did."

Then Navaro turned to Grace, gave her a hug, and told them what the doctor had said about his heart. "I'm gonna fucking start spending money like crazy!" he laughed, and Grace decided, contrary to prior judgment, that the man's life hadn't been lived in vain.

Eight hours later, Charlie and Grace pulled up to the house they'd rented, sight unseen, outside Tucson, Arizona, where nobody they knew had ever been.

Grace unpacked as the sun set across the desert, the fading pink light etching the ragged slopes of mountains in silhouette against the sky. She got up and stood in the back doorway, leaning against the jamb. Then she felt the heat of Charlie's presence and turned. He smiled, his shoulders looser, his posture more relaxed than it had been in a long time.

"How you doing?" he asked, and brushed a lock of hair from her eyes.

"Just fine."

The house was small and cozy, a ramshackle wooden cottage with an empty fenced-in front yard of desert scrub. There were no neighbors for miles, and the only signs of civilization were the telephone poles that ran alongside the little two-lane blacktop. It was a quiet place, Grace thought, isolated, where she could take off her clothes and run naked if she wanted. "Arizona? Are you *sure*?" her mother had asked. But Grace had never been this sure of anything before.

She took in the mountains, and drew a deep breath of desert air. Then she wrapped herself in Charlie's arms.

All day long, Grace had been too excited to eat, but then Charlie suggested a nighttime picnic to inaugurate their move. Great, she thought, a picnic. Charlie took the odds and ends of food they'd brought from Los Angeles, threw them in a shopping bag, and grabbed a bottle of wine.

They drove for a while into the desert, where the sky was filled with pinwheels of stars and the moon hung low and large. At the edge of a dry riverbed, Charlie stopped the car and consulted a particularly detailed map Grace hadn't even noticed he had.

"Where are we?" she asked.

Charlie flashed a strange grin and got out of the car. He spread a blanket and laid out the food.

After an hour, Charlie reached out his hand and led Grace into the riverbed, where, she noticed, the ground was broken in long jagged lines.

"What are we … ?"

Charlie didn't say a word. Instead, he consulted his watch, took her by the shoulders and positioned her precisely, putting his arms around her to make sure she didn't move.

In the desert chill, Charlie's warmth was nice against her skin. Grace felt her heat begin to rise. She leaned upward and kissed him, pressing into the curve of his body.

Then the air filled with rumbling, and the ground began to move and swell. "What the fuck?" Grace said.

"It's just a 3.3," Charlie told her. "But I thought it might be fun."

Slowly, the shaking stopped, and Grace felt herself thrust against him completely.

"Fun?" she said. "I know something else that's fun." She curled away a little, and reached for the buckle of his belt.

At home later, after Charlie was asleep, Grace lifted up the sheets and climbed quietly out of bed. Her skin gleamed silver in the moonlight, and she padded barefoot into the front room. The earthquake had set a charge in her, and she couldn't sleep. Maybe if I wrote about it, she thought, and picked up an old spiral notebook. She shivered at the touch of her naked back against the cold wooden chair.

For a moment, she stared at the page's empty lines. Then she cracked her knuckles and began.

"Los Angeles is the only major city in the world, thought Charlie Richter, heading east on Sunset in his red Rent-a-Corsica, where everybody has to drive. …"

APPENDIX

CHARLIE IN KOBE

Kobe, January 17, 1995

Dear Grandfather,

It was a beautiful night. That's the first thing, the thing no one will remember. The dawn was still an hour off and the stars sparkled in the winter sky like ice. There was a dusting of frost on the ground and my footsteps made a crunching sound when I walked into the park. As I set up my equipment my breath hovered before me in a cloud. It was so crisp and clear I began to doubt myself; back home in California, as you well recall, they talk about "earthquake weather" and how the ground starts shaking only when it's hot and dry. Then again, it hadn't been hot for Loma Prieta or for Northridge — just the dreadful symmetry of plates slipping, energy fields shifting, a force more powerful even than history.

The conference was a bust. All along, I knew it would be. But what else could I do but try? For weeks beforehand I'd had these nightmares, these *visions*, the city collapsing in slow motion to a soundtrack of piercing, knife-like screams. Every time I closed my eyes, it all came back again. So I thought, what the hell, your name is *Richter*. If anyone can make them listen, *you* can …

But they shouted me down and told me no one could predict an earthquake and that only a fool would try. What evidence did I have? How could I *explain* it? By telling them *you* were helping me? Verifying my findings and keeping me on track? These are men of science, after all, blind to anything that can't be proven, blind to anything suggesting the shadows behind the light. But you, Grandfather, you *are* the shadows. You may be dead but you are also living, tracelike, within this computer—your mind embedded in its circuitry, your ideas thrumming through its wires.

No, you are the one thing I can't explain. The one thing … So I walked out of that conference hall, went back to my hotel, and got ready to meet the dawn. I sat there, watching numbers scroll green and black across my screen. Five-forty-five a.m., January 17—virtually a year to the day since Northridge—the coincidence was striking. Evanrude had laughed when I announced the date, as if the whole thing were a joke or a cynical play for attention to predict a killer quake on the anniversary of another one.

But I knew it was coming. That night, in the hotel room, I saw buildings collapsing and heard the muffled roars of people trapped beneath the debris. Finally, I went down to the bar and drank a carafe of sake but, rather than calming me, it settled hot and sticky in my stomach and filled my throat with bile. At three a.m. I packed up my equipment: video camera, portable seismograph, infrared binoculars, laptop, electric lantern, and a folding camp chair. Now I could ride out the carnage, if my own excitement or the force of the tremor didn't shake me to the ground.

I remembered a moment as a boy, out walking with you, when you'd picked up a handful of gravel and told me, "This is the only thing that's real. Everything else is just wave form and energy, but this—is *solid*." And you let go of that gravel. We watched it fall through your fingers like lost time, spreading along the ground. That's why earthquakes fascinated you, because they represented solid matter turned fluid, but rather than seeing that as a contradiction, you said it just expanded our definitions of what solid and fluid really were. There was no reason solid states must be static; earthquakes merely illustrated the solidity of the earth reconforming itself. It was like a Gaia theory, the planet as living creature, even though you would never have admitted to believing in any idea as touchy-feely as that. As I looked for a place to observe the entire city, I thought about you, and asked you, and the earth, to keep me safe.

In the end, I settled on a field high up in the hills that ring Kobe—a deserted place with a panoramic view of the city and the harbor below. I arrived at exactly four-thirty-one, another coincidence—the time Northridge had exploded, exactly one year before. I parked on a service road, unloaded the trunk and trudged to the center of that field. I set the video camera on a tripod, hooked up the seismograph, lit the lantern, and lay everything else where I could reach it, when the time came.

The hour I spent waiting was one of the most wonderful in my life. All the anxiety of the preceding months left my body; there was no more wondering about how I'd tell the scientific community about this, what their reaction would be. I'd told them, and they hadn't believed me. The story had made the newspapers, and I'd been dismissed as yet another apocalyptic crank. What people didn't understand was that I was predicting not destruction but *change*, a larger picture, the image of a world in a state of solid flux.

And yet, sitting in my camp chair above the city, huddled into the bulk of my thick down coat for warmth, I fell under the spell of a most striking illusion—the permanence of reality, the immutability of matter, and the everlasting nature of all things. It was the stars that did it, I think, the same stars Dad used to study, sneering at your claims that the earth was all there is. I looked up and began to name the constellations— Big Dipper, Little Dipper, and the three sharp points of Orion's Belt. I remembered Dad telling me that, long after the earth had disappeared into the crucible of the sun, the stars would still be there, that it was just a conceit of yours, this importance of our world.

But now, I began to think the two things weren't mutually exclusive. My eyes moved from the stars to the lights of the night-wrapped city, to the twinkles of ship-light sparkling from the waters of the harbor, and I started to see how *they* were connected. I let my eyes go unfocused, and the boundaries disappeared. When I focused them again, I was struck by how solid everything looked, the trees fringing the perimeter of this field, the skyscrapers downtown, the four and five-story residential buildings in the city's sprawling neighborhoods. I picked up the binoculars and watched as neon signs flashed on and off throughout the city like heartbeats. An elevated highway ran along the lip of the shoreline, and train tracks, empty in the depth of night, cut a swath through the center of town. The night was so still and silent that the city seemed like an inevitability God had set into place, fully formed and complete. Thinking that, I began to doubt myself for the first time ...

And that's when it happened. The first rush was like a stutter, and after that everything moved like a dream. The trees around me began to spasm, and the lights of the city flared as transformers began to blow. Buildings shook and some of them fell. I was thrown, spread-eagle, across the grass—it was like being on the back of a beast, of an elephant running wild. I began to doubt gravity's existence, to think the earth itself might throw me. With the transformers went the lights, and then the quake shook my lantern to the ground, where it seemed to bounce in several directions at once, casting irregular beams of light across the field before me like a spastic searchlight. Beyond the narrow focus of its glow, the darkness was so thick it was surreal, as all the light in the world had been snuffed out. And yet, through it all, there were the stars ...

When the shaking finally ended, the stillness was intense. Not even the whisper of a ghost. From the city below came the screaming of car alarms, a million of them punctuating the horror of the night. I sat up, rubbed my eyes, felt around for my machines. I kept feeling the earth beneath me to make sure it was there. The video camera was still running, although it, too, had fallen, and the lens was dug face first in the dirt. I found the binoculars, turned them in the direction of the darkened city, where I saw the hot spots of newborn fires, and wisps of curling smoke rising to meet the sky. The elevated highway I'd noticed only minutes before had shaken onto its side; I looked at it once, twice, and a third time before I understood what I saw. All over Kobe, buildings were down, some in rubble, others slid akimbo halfway off their foundations. And the people, from this distance, were small as insects, swarming from the ruins into the streets.

I put down the binoculars, and lay out across the grass. It was cold, but my body had gone numb; it didn't matter anymore. For a moment, the thought flashed across my mind that it had happened as I'd predicted, that I was vindicated, that I was right. But then I remembered that elevated highway, down off its base like a child's plaything, and I thought less about the people who hadn't *listened* to me than those who'd never *heard*. By now, there were fires big enough to see with the naked eye, and sirens pulsing underneath the car alarms in a sharp and steady refrain. I tried to block the sounds out of my mind, but it was as if the night itself were screaming, and my entire body began to clench. I picked up the binoculars again, but it was too overwhelming. There was no such thing as scientific detachment anymore.

Instead, I found myself doing what my father might have done. I turned away from the earth and looked to the sky.

@unnamedpress

facebook.com/theunnamedpress

unnamedpress.tumblr.com

www.unnamedpress.com